The Ballad of

Sara Doom

*to Derek with Hope
from the Badlands*

— Hang Tough

Peace,

WHAT OTHERS ARE SAYING ABOUT THE BALLAD OF SARA DOOM

The Ballad of Sara Doom is a grab bag of thought-provoking stories, split-second challenges, glimpses of the sacred, and just plain fun. I recommend it for adolescents and adults alike, and all of us who are searching for spiritual meaning in the many culture zones we inhabit or visit. This is a timely and long overdue book for everyone interested in faith development and the creation of meaningful bridges between generations.

— Dr. Denise J. Doyle
Former Director of the Pastoral Institute
Incarnate Word College, San Antonio, TX

Sara Doom's search for her lost ethic is a dizzying eye-opening journey across a culture that seems to have misplaced its children along with its ethic. The "Ballad" recounting her journey is nothing less than a clarion call for our society—especially our churches—to hear the lamentations of our lost children. Only by really hearing them can we find them once again and, with them, our lost ethic and our future.

— Joe Patrick Bean
San Antonio *Express-News* columnist

Michael Harrington breaks new ground in his attempt to engage young people in a dialogue about the world they live in and especially the values at issue in that world. In a new and daring way, Harrington has adapted the allegorical, symbolic narrative long used in Christian literature. Sara Doom is a modern-day young pilgrim making her hesitant progress across our continent. I encourage those working with youth to examine this provocative experiment in speaking with the young.

— Michael Warren, Ph.D.
Professor, Department of Theology
St. John's University, Jamaica, New York
Author *Youth, Gospel, and Liberation*

Using images and language that speak to today's young people and their parents, Michael Harrington offers both generations a tool to open communication. *The Ballad of Sara Doom* enlightens parents about the world their children now face, while offering young people an understanding of the culture that prevailed while their parents were in their teenage years. In today's fragmented, rapidly moving world, we must find a way to stop, talk and most importantly listen…to each other and to our hearts. Sara Doom discovers our ethic is not "out there" among the many images and zones, but it is within.

— Deborah Knapp Bonilla
KENS TV News Anchor/Reporter—San Antonio

In the whispers of Michael's words and in the cries of the younger generation's voice rests the hope of God. Sara Doom is wandering and yet strikes poignantly at the heart, is set whimsically in the realm of reality and yet is prophetically profound, is on the edge and yet at the very core of the Gospel. The voice is worth reading…and heeding!

— The Reverend Ann E. Helmke
Evangelical Lutheran Church of America, Pastor
Director of The Peace Talks

HELLOOO...PLANET EARTH

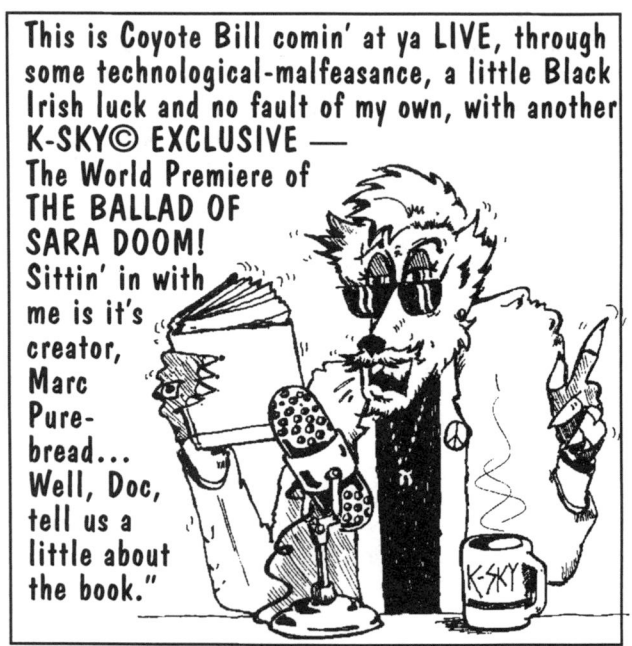

"This is Coyote Bill comin' at ya LIVE, through some technological-malfeasance, a little Black Irish luck and no fault of my own, with another K-SKY© EXCLUSIVE — The World Premiere of THE BALLAD OF SARA DOOM! Sittin' in with me is it's creator, Marc Pure-bread... Well, Doc, tell us a little about the book."

Look 'er, Mate. I know I'm just a Tasmanian marsupial ...but this book really hits me where I live!

Where's that—a *burrow?* Well, Doc, yer a success! Ya got the *Wombat* endorsement!

Um...Thanks, Hondo. I really didn't know anyone would actually READ it!

Well, SKY pilot, the Book says that a Prophet gets no respect in his own country, and you sure don't...so here's my advice... Preach hard, Rock steady, and Duck!"

The Ballad of

Sara Doom

Myths, Messages, and Markers From the Culture Zone

Michael O. Harrington

LANGMARC PUBLISHING

SAN ANTONIO, TEXAS

The Ballad of Sara Doom

MYTHS, MESSAGES, AND MARKERS
FROM THE CULTURE ZONE

by Michael O. Harrington

PUBLISHED BY
LANGMARC PUBLISHING
BOX 33817
SAN ANTONIO, TX 78265-3817

Library of Congress Cataloging-in-Publication Data in Process

ISBN 1-880292-13-0

DEDICATION

To my partner and my friend…
Janett, my love.
(Next stop, the Badlands …okay Skipper?)

MY GRADITUDE...

for my own Purebreads...

April, Justin, Roxie, Evan, Cody, Shea, Larkin, McLane, Teri, Tara, and to Blake.

You are a wonderful Nuclear Disaster.

...To Mandy "Angel" Kibler for being my model for Sara Doom. You are an angel, my friend.

...To Mindy Jones (for the "Quiet"), David Bearden (for Strider), John Goulas (for Lonesome Oak), Keliegh Reynolds (for smiling), Tara Schmid (for the mood), Karen Birdlebough (for Pooh), Chris Nevins (for "ologies"), Renée Tondre (for insanity), Jason Bulla (for Jobu), Jerry Wiggins (for "who whos"), Heather Goulas (for laughter), Leah Vann (for touch), and Carolyn Joiner (for courage), Steve Lancaster-Hall (for Heroes), Leia Jones (for the future), Suzanne Hall (for dance), Ann Helmke (for Dream Catchers), Brian Alderman (for music), and Lynn Alderman (for dolphins).

...To my sister Kathy and her guy Gary for taking us on the journey of a lifetime.

...To Mom and Dad for your imagination.

...To Michael Warren for introducing me to Culture Zones.

...To Paula Kummer (for musicals).

...To Jan and Henry Reed (for encouragement).

...To all the "weirdos" of this present culture who give time-journalers like me such great material (You know who you are).

...To the Reverend Dr. Jim Qualben for your history lessons and for introducing me to this art form.

...To Michael Qualben for taking me on a computer ride.

...And to my publisher, Lois Qualben...thanks for opening up my mind and motivation. What'll we do next?

...And many thanks, God, for your sense of humor.

CONTENTS

A DREAMCATCHER

PART I
THE PROBLEM WITH PROBLEMS

A CULTURE ZONE

PART II
MARKERS TO THE EXCELLENT THING

MARKERS

PREFACE
STONES SPEAK

VOICES. They are trapped in the ice-black air between mountain and plain in the Badlands of South Dakota. They hang in place like blasts of cold hard breath begging the silent stars for a home. Not quite listening, we can almost hear their tales of shattered native dreams. Shadows of angry dancers echo in forgotten firelight upon the canyon walls. And in piercing stillness the enormity of silence lurks like a ravenous wild animal awaiting dawn to begin the hunt.

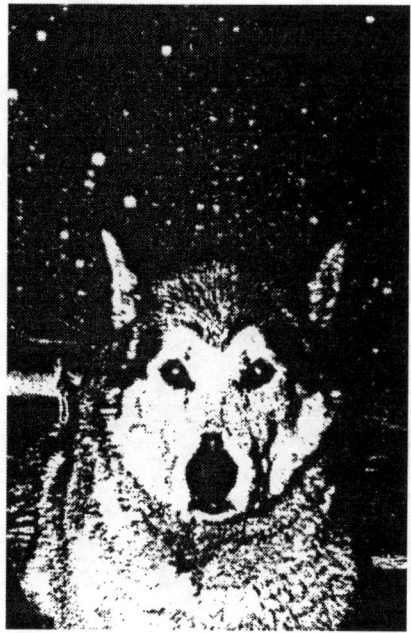

When I first heard the *Ballad of Sara Doom* (1990), it was but a faint whisper from the lips of this present generation, like stones speaking, figuring no one was listening. I consulted Marc Purebread (my mythical alter-ego). It was his encounter with Sara and her culture that spun this tale. Sara and Marc each take a journey. Each discovers something about the way the other views their generation.

Preceding each chapter in  Sara's journey, there is a mini-chapter that chronicles our storyteller as he criss-crosses the country trying to hawk his latest book. (Coincidentally, about teenagers, faith, ethics, and culture of the 90s).

> "
> And in piercing stillness is the enormity of silence, like a ravenous wild animal awaiting the dawn.
> "

REALITY CHECK!! Here I am, a 40-something white Protestant pastor-type; what in the name of Custer's ghost can I say about the culture, ethics, values or quality of this generation of young people? Forget the fact I've been about the business of "youth ministry" for 20-some years and am a husband of a sainted wife and the father of ten (yours-mine-ours-and-theirs). What is there left to say that is real—accurate—faithful—authentic or even readable?

And then the stones spoke to me.

> *"Let the voices of the lost guide themselves*
> *Their precious hearts are crying*
> *And already breaking free."*
>
> — *The Ballad of Sara Doom*

Now, that's cool. Is it possible that the past *still* has something to say to us today?

For longer than many parents and most "experts" realize, kids have been disconnected from the myths of manifest destiny, retirement-age rewards, lifelong two-parent nuclear family wholeness, career fulfillment, connections with history, and assumptions about a Christian culture, U.S.A.

As Sara would say, "I've lost my ethic and I don't know where to find it."

"

P.S. I call Sara's people the Silent Generation. But...*wait* until you hear what they have to say!

"

What myths have replaced them? MTV reasoning, wanton video carnage, single parent up-bringing, disintegrating social standards, careless acceptance of incivility, peer-reinforced mediocrity, and lowered expectations. Values systems that used to be considered normative have been rescinded for lack of interest.

As Sara would say, **"I'VE LOST MY ETHIC AND I DON'T KNOW WHERE TO FIND IT. "**

Sara begins her quantum leap search for her generation's lost ethic. Oh yes, Sara is an orphan who was adopted by a Native American medicine man from the Badlands of South Dakota. For many years, he has been teaching her the place her generation has in creation's plan.

Please don't take yourself too seriously or dissect too carefully the words painted on these pages. Sara would hate that. So, to a generation who has the toughest decision-making in all human history before you, I pray that you will see and hear *The Ballad of Sara Doom.* (You have the time.)

And the wilderness screams.

> *"There is a code of silence*
> *among Native American survivors, I suppose.*
> *It may be the hurt that comes from a trust that never was*
> *...or one long broken.*
> *Within this ancient quiet waits a secret hope.*
> *It trembles to awaken.*
> *Ageless as the Badlands' stones under a weary traveler's feet,*
> *the secrets of silence wait.*
> *Because they have no choice."*

> *"Oh listen, Spirit Master, to an ocean roar of stones.*
> *Like stars that fell to earth scattered without design.*
> *The children of this planet are becoming hard to find.*
> *From the Badlands of Dakota*
> *Sara Doom will soon see that*
> > *the eyes of all God's children*
> > *look just like you and me."*

— *The Ballad of Sara Doom*
Peace,
Mike

VOICES: Their voices are trapped among sounds of greed, video, hard rock, gun shots—yes, we can almost hear their tales of shattered dreams. And in piercing stillness an enormity of loneliness and frustration lurks, awaiting dawn to begin the hunt—the hunt for their ethic, their values, meanings, markers—and their God. The voices of the "Silent Generation." But...*wait* until you hear what they have to say!

The Publisher's Prelude
to the Purebread Parables

Why should you read this *Ballad*? Strictly for enjoyment! However, when you do, you'll never view our 90s youth culture in quite the same light as you did before you joined Sara and Marc on their adventures. Put your feet up, sit back and get to know two fascinating people. Sara and Marc represent very different generations and cultures. While Marc pokes fun at today's idols, Sara is truly mystified by them.

Who in the world is this Sara Doom person anyway? Sara is a teenaged orphan adopted at birth by her grandfather, Wally Skydancer, from the Badlands of South Dakota. Why should you want to get to know Sara—much less, travel with her? Why? Because you will see our 90s youth culture through new eyes—Sara's. She is gifted with eyes that *see* and ears that *hear*—and a heart of gold, a gentle spirit that is like a magnet for all sorts of people…and animals. She possesses the innocence of one who has been sheltered from TV, commercialism, and all that gory stuff. But she also has a curiosity and naiveté that drives her to take that quantum leap of faith into the unknown. Wally Skydancer has taught her many wise truths, but now he says it's time for her to seek her own messages, her own meanings and markers in search of an excellent thing—in search of her ethic and her most excellent thing, her God. (Sara read in Mr. Webster's dictionary that the word *ethics* means "the study of standards of conduct and moral judgment; moral philosophy; the code of morals of a particular philosopher, religion or group." So an "ethic" *must* be a *system* of ethics.)

Okay, so that's Sara. Who is this Marc Purebread fellow? In his forties, he has lived up to his armpits in the culture of the 60s *and* the 70s *and* the 80s, *and* now the 90s. He's a hard-working author who loves to write thought-provoking parables. He's experienced, somewhat cynical, but caring—especially about his family, his church, and young people. (That's why he wrote this book for and about them). Reflective as he can be with his chaotic schedule, Marc has apprehensive feelings about today's culture, its lack of interest in ethics, higher purposes, and positive role models. He talks a lot about culture zones in which adults and young folks often get "stuck."

> " Sara and Marc represent two very different generations and cultures. "

She is gifted with eyes that *see* and ears that *hear*—and a heart of gold.

I reject the notion that this younger generation is lazy, crazy, limited, over-stimulated, thankless, hapless, or (most significantly) silent.

Culture Zone

Dream Catcher

MARKERS: Borrowed from Moses
A sign of serious merit.

Culture Zone? Whaaaat? Whenever Marc sizes up a situation, he has this quirk of seeing people operating in a given culture zone. So, of course, he **names** each zone (and gives it a feather, wouldn't you know!). He does manage to offer us his often-satirical, yet sometimes-loving, definition of each zone, and he hangs a dream catcher by it. (Like most infants in her culture, Sara had a dream catcher hanging over her cradle. Its job was to catch and filter out the bad dreams and to catch the good dreams to reflect them back. The morning's sunlight reflects back *only* the good dreams. Now I see why Sara is always looking for the sun!)

Markers. There are ten markers (borrowed from Moses). Higher purposes, one might say. Something to strive for. Could a marker *possibly* be an ethic—or a value? One *could* consider it in that light.

And there are *quantum leaps* of faith. Sara joins a few other fairly strange characters as she leaps from there to here, here to there, from place to place, and time to time—an unusual geography lesson for us readers.

Drawings, photos, cartoons—Marc Purebread has a way with pen and pencil. When his frenzied life overflows with stressful happenings, his drawing pad becomes *his* "dream catcher." Purebread pictures paint a Purebread point!

Purebread Parables: Welcome to the land of "make believe" (laced with a little too much reality to satisfy a reader's comfort zone). A fable, a tale, a group of parables, one giant metaphor: each provides food for thought and discussion. *The Ballad of Sara Doom* is written for two age groups: younger and older! Two generations—yours and theirs. This story isn't to be taken too seriously—Sara and Marc would not like that!

Why would *anybody* want to publish a book about a mythical girl who communicates with dolphins and a not-so-mythical man who lectures to anyone who will listen—even to animals (yet isn't Dr. Doolittle?) Because it's great fun—and quite an excellent lesson—to close your eyes, take a quantum leap, and ponder some not-so-bizarre culture zones (and several caring discourses). Place your tongue in cheek and come along. *It'll be good for you!*

> *The Ballad of Sara Doom* is written for two age groups: younger and older!

> Place your tongue in cheek and come along. *It'll be good for you!*

Lois Qualben

— SARA PONDERS...
AND SHE SINGS...
EVER SO SOFTLY...

"I've lost my ethic and I don't know where to find it.
Maybe it lies beyond the Badland plain
knit together with the spirit of my sisters and brothers in far-
away lands.
If they've marked their way,
I'll see it through their eyes.
If their hearts cry...I will hear with my insides.
If an excellent thing exists...I will make it mine.

I'll miss you, Wally Skywalker.
...may your prayers for me be like the smoke from your fire as a
pleasing aroma into God's glorious night.
Hold me tight."

— The Ballad of Sara Doom

A search for spirituality, ingenuity and an ethic are markers of this generation.

SING THE PEPSI SONG

A latter 20th-century cultural analyst is kind of like a...well sorta like a...oh, an editorial cartoonist hooked on strong coffee and cigarettes pacing the kitchen floor late at night wondering if anyone really does care about much of anything...at all. One such Cartoonist-Writer and overwrought father found himself walking through Jerome, Arizona.

In 1899, Paul Hull said of the place, "It is the home of 19th-century cliff dwellers...buildings cling to the precipitous sides of the mountain-like swallow nests."

By the late 20th century, it was the artist colony home of many lost children of the 60s and other rainbow chasers. The Writer, his wife, his sister and brother-in-law were on their way from Flagstaff to Sedona. While they were stopped on a mountain road, a friendly flag woman gave them directions.

"I have a friend who bought his house up there for $300 while on an acid trip. Yep, there are lots of Granola People up there," she said.

There were. The Writer passed one of them who pointed to his shirt (which read, 'LIFE'S SHORT—PRAY HARD—READ THE BOOK).

"Great shirt, man, right on. As a matter of fact, this planet's life is short," he said.

One shop owner (she sold birds' nests) told them they could experience the cosmic convergence if **"We'll all hold hands and sing the Pepsi song."**

"

One shop owner (she sold birds' nests) told them they could experience the cosmic convergence if "We'll all hold hands and sing the Pepsi song."

"

The Writer stood in the sweltering sun, sipped a bottle of water (very chée-chée) and thought of *The Ballad of Sara Doom*.

"God's speed, Sara," was all he said.

 **ZONED OUT**
Culture Zone: Being with people as nutty as you feel.

THE PROBLEM WITH PROBLEMS IS THAT SOMEONE HAS TO TAKE A FIRST STAND.

I.E.: When your neighborhood is filled with children with empty bellies...someone needs to feed them...and that costs someone.

THE NAZARETH PROJECT

© Michael O. Harrington, 1994

The sun was going down over the Texas Hill County, and it made sad shadows appear through his study windows. The Writer stood and looked down at the itinerary on his desk and sighed, "I really don't want to go on this trip. Being away from Skipper and the kids just kills me."

One of his dogs was whining at his feet, sensing his melancholy. He picked up the dog and said,

"It's okay, Quizzer...I gotta go. See the sunset? There are too many sunsets out there. Too many orphans without much chance. They need for someone to hear their voice."

The old dog licked his face.

"Yeah, even from an old guy like me."

The Writer put down the dog, folded his itinerary, placed it in his briefcase and started to turn off the TV. The face of Radar O'Reilly from an old M*A*S*H* rerun was playing in the VCR. He paused for a moment on the image and said, "God's speed."

GOD'S-SPEED ZONE

Culture Zone: Every journey begins with a friendly mix of foolishness and courage. Each mission has a noble reason to begin. But it helps to feel that you won't be on your own.

PART ONE

THE PROBLEM WITH PROBLEMS

"Calling to the Quiet"

It was like the mouth of a crypt with canyon walls. Along the treacherous road descending from Flagstaff, Arizona, to Sedona, faces of the Navajo Nation lived in the rock. Still and silent. Unnoticed by campers and tourists, those faces watched and waited.

Sedona has become a camp meeting of Harmonic Convergence-channeling, psychic gypsies, New Age light seekers, cosmic carpetbaggers—all of them hoping to grab some spiritual booty from Native American life treasures.

Reaching out my hand,
I find you.

— Mindy
"

The Writer read one brochure that claimed to be an "Earth Wisdom Vortex Tour" complete with ancestral Native American Medicine Wheel secrets, a mish-mash of myth and science and unsolicited guidance. He shook his head. All around him were castles, guard towers, and temples hewn into monuments of red sandstone.

"Vortex Tours," he mumbled.

And he thought of a young woman who had told him another tale.

"Trust is a deadly weapon
Killing the innocent of hearts.
Love is the cure to the wounds
Understanding stands apart.

Fear surrounds my life
Only needing to be loved.
Reaching out my hand,
I find you."

© Mindy Jones, '92

"Someone is calling to you, Sara Doom," he said.

  **ALONE ZONE**

Culture Zone: Being alone, but not really.

A MOMENT ON THE MOUNTAIN
...THE PROBLEM WITH ETHICS
(IS THERE MORE THAN SITUATIONAL ETHICS?)

Somewhere in the Badlands of South Dakota, an abandoned teenaged girl is about to begin the journey of a lifetime.

And like all such quests, her situation is desperate.

"Please tell me, Wally Skydancer. Where is the source of human kindness?

Beyond the mountains, is there life on the information highway?

From moment to moment is anything constant left?

Does a Right still live anywhere out there?

Skydancer, do people *not* want to die?"

Somewhere between the Badlands of South Dakota and a Black Hole, *The Ballad of Sara Doom* begins.

> **"The problem with Situational Ethics is they suppose each moment to be unique and unaccountable to eternity."**
> — Wally Skydancer

 NOW ZONE
Culture Zone: Being in the moment when whatever you do is okay.

"CALLING TO THE QUIET—PART II"

"It's raining like a fool here in Chicago. Yeah, I know. Probably another layover, again. Kiss all the kids for me. Uh-huh. I love you," he said as he replaced the receiver on a pay phone hook.

The Writer looked around the confusion of humanity in an awful hurry from there to here. O'Hare Airport is the place to be for that, he thought.

Airport coffee tastes like haste, but he drank it anyway and watched the faces of the sad, the mad, the anxious, the obnoxious, the mysterious, and the lost pass by in endless futility. All their planes are socked in; what's the rush, he wondered. He took the poem out of his briefcase and looked at its frayed pages, again.

> *"Calling to the quiet,*
> *Screaming out in pain*
> *Wanting help and contact*
> *Where's the light?*
>
> *Not knowing where I'm headed*
> *Where is my broken path?*
> *Show me the way home.*
> *Where are you, God?"*

© Mindy Jones, '92

"Where are you, God?"

Just then he caught a glimpse of a frail teenaged girl with a rucksack over her buckskin jacket. "Sara Doom," he thought.

  **ZERO ZONE**

Culture Zone: Being less than Zero and searching for a God out there.

THE SOUTHSIDE OF CHICAGO IS THE BADDEST PART OF TOWN

... THE PROBLEM WITH ABSOLUTES (IS THERE GROUND FOR ABSOLUTES?)

> **The problem with Absolutes is you have to stand your ground to notice them.**
>
> — Skydancer

Late at night after a rock concert, somewhere on the University of Chicago quadrangles, Sara encounters an angry young man. She's unaware he's the band's vocalist. Throughout the night, the two cross paths with many absolutely commanding individuals, until…Eddie says,

> *"Sara! Wake up and smell the gunpowder!*
> *Everything changes.*
> *Everything!*
> *Nothing can stay the same, forever.*
> *But, brother Eddie . . . (says Sara)*
>   *the wind always lifts the eagle's wings,*
>   *and even snow cannot take the glow from a*
>   *friend's smile."*
>
> — *The Ballad of Sara Doom*

Standing by the Stagg Field monument to the first atomic chain reaction, Sara's voice calls to the darkness.

> *"Even so…the mind of man cannot comprehend*
> *the mind of God…*
> *the mind of love…"*
>
> — *The Ballad of Sara Doom*

-HELP!

Sara looked up and saw a banner hanging outside the Divinity School building. It read, "Nuclear-Free Zone." Across the street was the Club NO EXIT. "HELP!" was all she said.

The journey continues.

(*The problem with Absolutes is you have to stand your ground to notice them.* — Skydancer)

 **NUCLEAR-FREE ZONE**

Culture Zone: The sense that Nuclear Disaster is not just a bygone theory and making yourself feel better by thinking it's gone.

> Even so…the mind of man cannot comprehend
>   the mind of God…
>   the mind of love…
>
> — Sara

"CAN YOU BELIEVE THESE KIDS TODAY... NO RESPECT FOR NO..."

"

Knowing what to do...
Wanting to wait...
Knowing it will hurt...
Waiting to change."

— Mindy

He shook his head, "Why me?" he howled to himself. "Stuck in New York's LaGuardia Airport, snowing like a madman outside. As if the ten-hour layover in Chicago wasn't bad enough, I'm standing next to a woman who hasn't taken a breath since she started her verbal assault on teen-agers over an hour ago."

"What's the use?" he wondered.

The Writer walked over to the pane glass window and watched the snow fall relentlessly upon the planes, which sat like toys strewn by an angry giant on the tarmac below. He could still hear the end of the young woman's song in his memory.

"If you're listening to my cries,
Why do they grow louder?
I'm afraid of giving up.
Are you out there?

Knowing what to do...
Wanting to wait...
Knowing it will hurt...
Waiting to change."

© Mindy Jones, '92

Oh, how he wished he were home. Then in the window's re-flection, he saw the walnut-complexioned young woman who sat near him on the flight. She looked more lost than before, and then she was gone.

"Knowing what to do, Sara...Knowing it will hurt," he said.

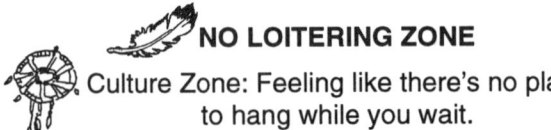

NO LOITERING ZONE
Culture Zone: Feeling like there's no place
to hang while you wait.

HEY LOOK KIDS, IT'S MEATLOAF!

...THE PROBLEM WITH LANGUAGE (IS IT SOMETHING I SAID?)

A series of misadventures led our heroine to a snow-showered street called 42nd. Near Times Square and the Theater District, garish sleeze pandered to tourists' expectations, all punctuated by natives' streetwide rudeness. To avoid frostbite ("I can't believe it's colder here than in Dakota"), Sara follows a crowd into the old Ed Sullivan Theater where the David Letterman Show has begun taping the night's silliness.

A thin, impeccably dressed man with a shock of curls and a Terry Thomas gap between his teeth waves a stack of index cards above his head. The crowd roars approval.

"That's right, kids, I have in my hand tonight's Top Ten List from the home office in Sioux City."

The cheers are nearly deafening. Sara is confused.

"Top ten questions a teenager might ask the Pope."

Thinking it is a question-and-answer show, Sara stands and cries out,

"I've lost my ethic. Do you know where I can find it?"

A hush falls over the crowd. The host shoots his producer a dumbfounded look. Sponsors grit their teeth. Moving like a spider monkey through primordial ooze, the host leads Sara to the stage. He invites her to read tonight's Top Ten List.

"But, I don't understand these words, sir."

"It's okay," he whispers, "neither do they. So just make up your own."

The music plays on with MeatLoaf screaming, **"What about your future? It's defective."**

" Top ten questions a teenager might ask the Pope.
— Letterman

" **"The problem with language is the assumption that everyone cares what we say."**
— Skydancer **"**

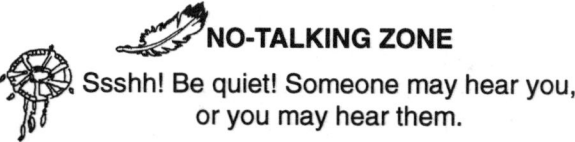
NO-TALKING ZONE
Ssshh! Be quiet! Someone may hear you, or you may hear them.

"Twelve Minors Arrested in Prostitution Ring…"

"They went that-a-way, Baby!"

GRAND CENTRAL…AIN'T SO GRAND

"I'm sorry the kids were disappointed. When I got to the theater, they told me that since my flight was delayed, they had to replace me. Yeah, I know…I was replaced by MeatLoaf singing *Life is a Lemon, And I want my Money Back*. Anyway, I'm sure the kids enjoyed that more than old Dad's book. By the way, did you catch that young girl from the audience? I think we know her. Anyway, I'm here at Grand Central Station…I'm on standby to Princeton. Maybe by morning I can be there for the conference. Who knows. Kiss the kids…love you. Bye, bye," he said and hung up the phone.

The Writer found a not-so-comfortable bench and opened the *New York Times*. From the corner of his vision, he thought he saw the young woman from the Letterman Show being escorted by an old Black Pullman porter. Were his eyes playing tricks on him? They seemed to be stepping onto an old steam locomotive. But then, it was gone. He glanced back at the *Times* and read, "Twelve Minors Arrested in Prostitution Ring…" He looked at the snowy distance and thought he heard—

"Run, Sara, run…
To the sound of the drum,
Beating in your heart ♪ ♫
…Sara, Run."

— *The Ballad of Sara Doom*

 **END ZONE**
Culture Zone: The running-away-to feeling
and feeling you're not getting there.

"This Doesn't Look Like Kansas, Toto"

...The Problem With What is Acceptable (What is the basic ethical stuff?)

Poor Sara. Escorted back onto 42nd Street by zealous CBS pages (because she had gotten bigger laughs than Dave), she was once again in the storm. "Oh Skydancer, is there somewhere in the world where it *isn't* snowing?"

As luck would have it (if you believe in such magic), Sara is about to be shown the town through the old train's windows by an odd little band of New Yorkers who are known as the Roundball Dancers. Although the RB Dancers aren't listed under "Tour Guides" in the yellow pages, their style of sightseeing is just what the medicine man ordered.

"Scuse me, Ms. Doom...but just what do you think is acceptable?"

"Besides you guys? I'm still looking. But, where does this train go?"

> *"Into the night fog. Away from the despair.*
> *Out to a foreign country.*
> *Not in the city. Who knows? Why? Who Cares?"*
> — *The Ballad of Sara Doom*

"It may not be snowing there. May the angels of the eagle be with you, my brothers. Adios," Sara said after unmarked time had passed.

And the lonesome rail cries.

The problem with what is acceptable is that basic ethical stuff like respect and human kindness is hard to accept.

— Skydancer

"

"Yo...Ms. Doom. You think *this* is bad, wait'll ya see Jersey."

KANSAS ZONE

Culture Zone: You know, this really doesn't look like Kansas any more, Toto.

"IT IS ALL RELATIVE, YOU KNOW"

His grandfather had attended Princeton at the turn of the century. That is what it felt like as he walked her antique halls. The Writer had attended the conference, and the book was well received, but something tugged his memory. He stood outside his favorite coffee shop and lit his pipe. What is it, he thought. In the glow of the lighter on the window, he did a double take. A very familiar young woman was sipping cocoa with old Albert Einstein's ghost. But it seemed as real as his wife's embrace. He could almost hear them say,

"Does history really repeat itself, Al?"

"Absolutely! But vat good does it do to do all zat repeating if zose in ze present dilemma do not find it relevant?"

"…History likes to live right under your fingernails like sod zat von't vash away. But, if one iss in a hurry, it iss merely a nuisance. It iss easy to vash your hands of it. It iss more time absorbing to insist on eternity."

"But, what of my lost ethic?"

"Vell, dis cocoa iss almost gone, but zers anudder pot a-brewin. It iss all relative, you know."

The Writer did another double take, and they were gone.

"It's all *relative,* you know?"

It is more time absorbing to insist on eternity.   — Einstein

 GET-REAL ZONE

Culture Zone: That feeling you get with your people when it's hard to tell if what *really* happened *really* matters.

PARDON ME, MR. EINSTEIN?

...THE PROBLEM WITH WHAT IS ETERNAL
(ARE WE TOTALLY DISCONNECTED FROM HISTORY?)

The old depot at Princeton Station hasn't been used in years, yet a phantom train with one lone passenger and a Pullman porter named Mercury just arrived. It was like something from a scene in one of those marvelous black and white movie mysteries. A curious customer on a life-long ride. From there to here. Ending their journey in history.

The campus of Princeton University was more exquisite than her postcards showed...more inviting than Ivy League lore...ever growing from the forest primeval...more enchanting than a child's tale...foreboding, as well, like a projection from some timeless source.

Walking beneath the splendor of those structures for classical learning, Sara Doom feels like she's in a dream. No one seems to notice either her or friendly Mercury. No one, save a quizzical old gentleman with a tattered cardigan and electric hair. Barely able to see his lips move under a walrus-like mustache, Sara is entranced.

"Do you luff hot cocoa, young lady? Good. Dere iss dis cafe, of sorts, on ze Main zat is often generous in zeir portions. And da fire iss varm. Could you und...Mr. Mercury? Yes, of course. Vould you mind showing me ze way?"

"But, Mr...um..."

"Einstein...please, but call me Al."

"But, Mr. Al, how do we know where your cafe is? I've lost my ethic and can't even find *that*."

Through that historic grin he says, "Oh, zat's all right, young lady. So have ve all. Ve've lost it in details und built a monument zu its refuse. Never mind dough. I'm sure you can lead us zu our destination. You'll just love ze flavor of it all."

Just then the snow stopped falling and the slightest glint from a dying star caught Sara's eye.

>
> " Oh, zat's okay, young lady...so have ve all. Ve've lost it in ze details...und built a monument zu its refuse. Never mind though...I'm sure you can lead us zu our destination; you'll just love ze flavor of it all.
> — Einstein "

🪶 **TWILIGHT ZONE**

Culture Zone: That uneasy sense that what is eternal is too far away, and what is history never happened.

"Will this affect my tip, Boss?"

"I'm the one who needs a tip…"

*"Thank you, Great Father Spirit.
Thank you for one more day."*

*And Mercury led the way.
No one else even noticed.*

—The Ballad of Sara Doom

DEATH GRIP ON REALITY

A local Raleigh-Durham talk show host shook The Writer's hand.

"Great segment! Just great! Sorry I can't chat, but my next guest is the Reverend Jesse Jackson, and we don't want to keep Jesse waiting…"

His voiced trailed into the ridiculousness of his tie, so The Writer smiled and walked off stage. He asked a page to call him a cab to the airport and overheard Jesse say,

"What do you mean, we only have 15 minutes left? You gave that Writer five. My time is valuable, sir, and I have much to say on the subject of…"

His voice disappeared into the host's gleaming smile. The writer enjoyed that and left. He spoke to the driver, someone named Rom-duck-tor,

"You know the problem with Values, um, Rom-duck-tor?"

"That is Rom-duck-tor, Boss. No, no, I don't have no valuables, Boss," the driver said nervously.

"Well, the problem with Values is…
while the bad ones are overrated,
the good ones ain't for sale," The Writer said.

"Will this affect my tip, Boss?"

"Rom-duck-tor…Why is it that the valueless stuff has a death grip on our reality?"

"I don't know, Boss. I just drive cab. See?"

"Um, yes…you just drive cab, but I'm the one who needs a tip," The Writer mused, watching sleet glaze the window.

 **NO-PARKING ZONE**

Culture Zone: Here's a tip—when everything feels worthless, make sure nobody's trying to pick your pocket.

TIPPER, THIS IS JESSE. JESSE, THIS IS TIPPER. TIPPER. JESSE. THIS IS A VALUE.

... THE PROBLEM WITH VALUES (WHAT IS VALUABLE ANYWAY?)

Mercury has requisitioned yet another train. Leaving Al Einstein waving in the distance, the track bears them into the latter 20th century. Without a ticket and being rather ravenous, Sara searches for the club car. Passing through the sleeper cars, her eyes become heavy. Wondering what will happen next, Sara slips uneasily into a REM state.

Voices of muttered conviction jolt Sara like the crackle of fussin' cockateals. Not really wanting to look, Sara slightly opens her right eye. Seated on a plush velvet Victorian settee is an immaculately tailored *Good Housekeeping* cover girl. She sips English tea without smearing her lipstick or her Doris Day smile. Shifting her gaze to Sara, she winks her butterfly lashes. Sara, terrified, shuts her eyes.

She peeks uneasily through her left eye. Perched on an antique deacon's bench, an ebony man with flashing hyperthyroid eyes and flashier threads is assailing the blond Mrs. America across a teak tea table. In an extravagant gesture of massive hands, he catches Sara in his rivoting gaze. Grin intact, he bellows, "Keep hope alive!"

Sara notices Mercury is serving refreshments, and she catches her breath. The Barbiesque woman speaks. "Just look at this child, Reverend Jackson. Look what the lack of Family Values has done to her. Are you hungry, dear? Crumpet? Croissant? Scone?"

"Why feed her cake when she cries for soul food? Can't you see, madam…she has no Values…you stole them from her. Can someone say Amen?"

Approaching the feast-laden table, Sara sighs, "Oh yes, ma'am. Do you have my ethic? I'm so hungry, I nearly forgot I had lost it. I'll gladly buy it back. How much is it worth, ma'am? *Amen.*"

 **TRUE-VALUE ZONE**

Culture Zone: The feeling you get with a left and right hook. Duck!

" Why feed her cake when she cries for soul food? Can't you see, madam…she has no Values…you stole them from her. Can someone say Amen?   — Jesse "

" Why, everything in this coach is beyond Value, dear.   — Tipper "

32

> **The problem with values is like trying to buy something of high quality: the cost may be tremendous.**
>
> — Skydancer

"Everything in this coach is beyond value, dear." —Tipper

"Except you…of course." —Jesse

"Of course."

Beyond Hope, passing Good Taste, through Shenendoah, toward Florida the coach rocks on.

"I GUESS THAT QUALIFIES THAT!"

> Can you just sign mine: 'All my love, Mickey Mouse'?

Am I a writer or just another hack, he wondered. Here am I having breakfast with Snow White, signing books for people who don't read them. I happen to be part of their Quality Entertainment Experience that will live in their memory about as long as it took for the ink to dry from my signature. Oh, well, it pays the bills…I guess that qualifies that, he thought.

He remembered his phone call home that morning. He had spoken with his 18-year-old son. "Yeah, I got an 1180 on my SAT, but I'm not even going to contact any more colleges till I bring it up another 100 points," he had told his dad.

I guess that qualifies *that*, he thought.

Snow White whispered that she was going out for a cigarette when a sunburned woman asked him, "Can you just sign mine: 'All my love, Mickey Mouse'?"

I guess that qualifies *that!*

"C'mon, Snow, …let's blow!"

 NO-SMOKING ZONE

Culture Zone: The odd perspective that all which separates your section from the Smoking Zone is an outstretched arm holding a lit match.

"SHAQ SLAMS THE MOUSE"

...THE PROBLEM WITH QUALITY (WHAT QUALIFIES WHAT?)

Being a part of a forever-night means never having to say, "I'm surprised." When Sara found herself at Disney World in Orlando, she wasn't surprised. When she was met by a five-foot duck, she wasn't distressed. Arm wrestling with Cinderella was no surprise. Counting countless techno-created realities was tiring, but not surprising. Even seeing an internationally-acclaimed ice skater tell Goofy he was goofy didn't seem too silly. But when she saw a man-mountain African-American going one-on-one with an overstuffed Mouse on the Disney back lot blacktop basketball court...*surprise* would be an understatement.

Approaching some dwarf, she exclaimed, "Um, Mr. Dwarf?"

"Dopey. Dopey Dwarf."

"That's a sad name, Dopey."

"I know. To be politically correct, I'm changing it to Unqualified Idiot of Marginalized Height."

"Um, Dopey...What is it with the big Mouse and bigger dark-skinned man with earrings?"

"They're qualifying for the Disney Dunk Finals."

"But is it necessary for them to be so rude and pretend they're so wonderful all at the same time?"

"Sure lady, it's a prerequisite."

So on into the night it goes. Slamming, taunting, sneering, cursing, general mayhem and macho stuffing. The ceaseless petitions for foul play streaming from the mass of spectators made one thing clear to Sara. "No one seems to know what makes this (or anything) so."

Dunking the fat mouse through the hoop, the large slamdunker replied, "Chaos is too overwhelming for most folks...so they look to dudes like me for Style."

> Chaos is too overwhelming for most folks...so they look to dudes like me for Style. —Shaq

DISNEY MOMENT ZONE

Culture Zone: The feeling that things are as goofy as you are dopey.

Standing at the Disney gate, Sara hears the wind blowing from the Badlands of Dakota as the wolf warns the moon.

"That's the problem with problems, isn't it?
The loss of that one clear character…
That understanding of what makes us free…
We've misplaced our excellent things."
— *The Ballad of Sara Doom*

> **The problem with Quality is that mountain air is sweeter, but Calvin Klein is more accessible.**
> —Skydancer

(Thus ends Part One of *The Ballad of Sara Doom*.)

"THE CLOAK OF DECEMBER"

> To hope against hope,
> that birthing happens…
> Beneath the cloak.

Sara was so sure it was all just some awful dream. Always darkness...forever night...people pretending that they no longer need the light..

And no one saying...
So few praying...
No one believing it was all right.
So she remembered the Badlands' snow, and waited.
Sara knew the time to stand was near.
She sang to Jesus...
because she'd heard *he* might hear.

"The snow came down peaceful...
gentle...
As the clouds broke up in
frozen tears...
Quiet they came upon the
unquenchable fire
of all her human fears.

The hard ground waits
and accepts the cloak of December.
Beneath each flake, crystal...unique...
the unmovable ground becomes Earth.
To hope against hope,
that birthing happens...
Beneath the cloak."
— *The Ballad of Sara Doom*

 **FREEZE ZONE**

Culture Zone: When everything is kind of frozen in time
so you can feel a little safer.

PART TWO

MARKERS
TO THE
EXCELLENT
THING

"ONE GOD, SILENT AS THE DESERT"

With measured indifference, the sun surveyed the high desert and wondered,

"Where are all the buffalo?

They were here just a moment ago."

She radiated uneasily now. Seeing the ant-like parade of vehicles, she considered vaporizing them with a blink of an eye, but decided just to grow very, very...cold.

"Where are the Hopi, the Apache, the Navajo Nations," she said.

Dolphins once lived here,
and the stories they told...
of one...
Silent...God.

"...the Hualapai, Comanche, and Papago?
These...
the sons and daughters of earth and sky
...and where is Sara Doom?
She was sent to become one, and protect the sun...
Silent as the Mohave.

Listen in the waves of burning cold,
Dolphins once lived here,
and the stories they told...
of one...
Silent...God."

—The Ballad of Sara Doom

ENDANGERED-SPECIES ZONE

Culture Zone: Feeling identified with those whose existence is terminal.

A DIALOGUE WITH A DOLPHIN
...WHO'S IN CHARGE HERE?

Totally put off by her own species, Sara Doom heads for the beach. Still believing endless night will break into glorious day, she sits upon a surf-bathed rock and decides to stay. "Until I'm so moved, I will not move."

"Good point, child," notes a passing dolphin, adding, "Problem is, most of your kind don't know who's in charge."

"Problem is, Mr. Fish, My Kind are mostly dead."

"Dolphin . . . not Fish . . . a cetacean by trade."

"Sorry."

"Common mistake. One must be clear on the facts to make things clear."

"But I'm puzzled. My species doesn't appear to care who's in charge."

"Little wonder. Your species has too many gods."

"How many is *too* many?"

"I'd say five billion is a bit excessive."

"Whose should we choose?"

"That's your problem. Isn't it?"

> **MARKER 1**
>
> There is one God.
> There is one you.
> Get to know each other.

> "Until I'm so moved, I will not move."
>
> —Sara

> "Little wonder. Your species has too many gods."
>
> —Dolphin

DOLPHIN-SAFE ZONE

Culture Zone: Those rare times and places where it's safe to question even God.

THE IDEAL, IDEA

The Writer turned off the cellular phone and handed it back to the limo driver.

"Rats!" was all he said aloud but, inside, his mind reeled.

> "I've changed my mind…Hey, I can do that; I'm a sensitive guy… anyway…I have this idea…"

"You'd think that once on this trip I could catch a break. But NO, if it's not raining, it's snowing…if you're late to Letterman, there's always Meat Loaf…people would rather have Mickey Mouse's autograph than yours…Sheesh! And now…NOW, my publicist wants me to speak at Graceland. I mean, for pity-sweet sake…*Graceland,* home of the last great idol of Baby Boomer fantasies."

He looked out of the window as the limo passed the Memphis Pyramid. They weren't going slow enough, but he thought he saw a familiar young woman in conversation with an even more familiar man. The Writer smiled. He dialed the phone and spoke.

"Listen, Quince, I have an idea…yeah, I know…I was steamed about the Graceland thing, but I've changed my mind…Hey, I can do that; I'm a sensitive guy…anyway…I have this idea…"

Onward through the Memphis night they drove. Onward to Graceland. He was excited as the idea unfolded. In his heart he heard her song.

"It may not be ideal
To let your idols burn…
But if we give ourselves a chance
We might not miss our turn."

—The Ballad of Sara Doom

NO IDOLIZING ZONE

Culture Zone: It's a quiet place where you shut off your engine long enough to get a good idea.

"ELVIS HAS JUST LEFT THE BUILDING"

...WHO'S THE IDOL?
("LOVE ME TENDER")

What makes a quantum leap? Theoretically speaking, it might be one unit (one thing) that has within it the smallest quantity of energy that can exist independently. Sara, being one such unit, closes in on an ancient mystery. Planted firmly before a massive pyramid, she considers her mistake.

"This doesn't look like Egypt."

"Makes sense," replies an overweight, middle-aged man sitting on a park bench. "This is Memphis...Tennessee."

"Figures. Make a quantum leap of faith and you take your chances."

"Been my experience, little lady. What are ya'll looking for?"

"My ethic. I seem to have lost it."

"Think ya'll will find it in that there monument to futility?"

"What god was it designed for, sir?"

"Basketball, I think. Don't know, but it sure wasn't built to worship me."

"Pardon me, sir, but do people worship in there?"

"Well heck yeah, they do. People will worship any old thing they can put in a box and take home to their closets."

"But that doesn't seem very reverent, sir."

"What's reverence got to do with idolizing, missy?"

"What indeed?" Sara mumbles as she walks away.

"Where ya'll gonna leap-faith to now?"

"The Badlands. The Desert. Somewhere where people don't make idols...I don't know."

"I don't either, but if ya'll keep walkin' that way, all ya'll will find is the Mississippi Delta."

"A barren land?"

"God forsaken."

"Good."

MARKER 2

Idols are very heavy things. If you have to carry one around...you'll be exhausted before you start.

"

What's reverence got to do with idolizing, Missy?   — Elvis

 **PYRAMID ZONE**

Culture Zone: Even ancient structures sometimes leave one feeling God-forsaken.

THE NAME OF THE PROPHET

The Writer was sitting in the Memphis airport having coffee with his best friend from seminary. Classmates had nicknamed his friend Lonesome Oak because he grew up in Arkansas' Mississippi Delta, and he was big as an oak— the tallest thing for miles around. Lonesome had been late to their brief reunion because, as he put it, "Yep, had to give that young gal a lift. Why, she and some old Black gentleman were just walkin' down that side road like they didn't have better sense. Dropped 'em at Peabody station house, an' told the dispatcher to give 'em some help. Crazy gal looked like an Indian. Whoa, can you imagine what the locals woulda done with that pair?"

The Writer told Lonesome about this idea he had tried at his Graceland gig.

"It's just an idea, but what if we had an internship for college students to work within their generation. You know, work in the public school system, the churches, even in the streets. Kinda work it like the Peace Corps, but the mission field is right here at home…but, no government stuff or para-church interference…"

> "
> Kinda work it like the Peace Corps, but the mission field is right here at home…

Lonesome refilled his pipe and chuckled.

"Still tryin' to be a prophet, old chum?"

"No, really Oak. It would give them ownership, a cause…a sanctuary…I even thought up a name— **"Culture Zone."**

Lonesome Oak put his meaty hand on his friend's shoulder.

"Yeh, y' gotta have a name to git started," he said.

 **CULTURE ZONE**

Culture Zone: You are the prophets of your generation, naming your mission and creating your sanctuary.

"I KNOW I'VE GOTTA NAME"

...DON'T TAKE IT FOR NOTHING.

Lonely roads. They lead from nowhere to nothing, or from Memphis to the Mississippi Delta, sometimes. Along the way—that's the kind of feeling she had. Are we always along the way from nowhere to nothing? If not, why do we appear so fearful of others or of ourselves? Questions gallop on.

Against the lapping waters of a lumbering Mississippi, a chorus of tiny voices creases the gloomy morning air.

"Voices!" Sara exclaims. "Children's voices! The dawn must be near."

She could see the clapboard schoolhouse now. It stood like a shaky fortress against the night. Sara approached it and opened the door. The delighted voices of a cache of young Black children greeted her.

"Good morning, Starshine!"

Sara moved to the back of the room and sat silently, wearily, behind an old desk. The children smiled. One ventured forward and said,

"My name is Charity. What's yours?"

"Doom."

> **MARKER 3**
> No one else has your name.
> It isn't Sally or Joe...
> It is your Soul.

NO NAME ZONE
Culture Zone: Without a name—you're nothing.

"Good morning...

Starshine!"

"My name is Charity..."

"Voices!"

42

AN OPEN LETTER TO AND FROM THE "UNSEEN CHILDREN'S CHURCH"
by Marc Purebread

Asleep. New Orleans—the Big-Easy—bastion of Southern civility with a touch of Zydeco music and Cajun charm, was asleep.

It was Sunday morning in the Big Easy, and almost everyone was still asleep. The Writer wrote. He wrote to an unseen church, an invisible generation, as free of time as jazz, and just as beautifully discordant. He wrote. And, he hoped that some day, somewhere, someone from this unknown generation would remember the day they were liberated and began to tell their story. ("Maybe today," he thought.)

Standing in the pulpit of the cathedral that keeps watch over Jackson Square, the words he wrote, he spoke…

The rest of us must choose whether we are going to be *creative* enough, and *open* enough, and *real* enough to these young men and women, before we can ask them to join us in the contemporary church.
"

"Please don't run screaming into the night. You get to choose the stuff you want to be involved in, and the stuff that is meaningful to you. Where you want to go, you go.

"Before we can ask them to join us in the contemporary church, the rest of us have to choose whether we are going to be *creative* enough, and *open* enough, and *real* enough to include these young men and women. To a place that will hear *their* voice, and give *them* access, and meet some of *their* needs, they *will* come. These could appear to be very impressive and very impossible goals for today's church. It will be a stretch for those who are outside the Unseen Children's Church.

"We have let them down if they think, 'I can't wait to get out of here.' If they say to themselves, 'This is all just so *boring*. What is all this church stuff about? What's it saying to me? It isn't that big of a deal!' No matter how special we make the day, it will remain a NON-event—IF it is not as special to them as being on the honor roll at school—IF it is not as special as being on a city championship soccer team or softball team—IF it is not as special as hanging out on the street corner, or even sneaking into an R-rated movie. For them a rite of passage into the church will not stack up with other growing events in their lives. We have missed something along the way.

"They are on the road to Emmaus with us. We are two believers who have gone from Jerusalem to Emmaus and are talking together and worrying because, to us, Jesus is still dead.

"Jesus appears to us on the road. He talks to us. He teaches us, and we still don't know who He is.

We are two believers who have gone from Jerusalem to Emmaus and are talking together and worrying because, to us, Jesus is still dead.
"

"We spend a lifetime bumping into religious things. Most of us have had enough Sunday School and youth groups and confirmation classes. But we are two people on the road to Emmaus from Jerusalem, and we assume Jesus is dead. The Unseen Children's Church may be under the impression that He is not alive because He is not alive to *us*, not creative to *us.* He appears to hold little meaning for us. (We may also be under that same impression.)

"The slight hope we leave ourselves is that all our God stuff someday might become an experience helpful enough to us and important enough to us that it might be at *least* as important as what we are going to wear tomorrow when we go to school, or at *least* as important as what is on MTV. And at *least* as important as how we look when we go to the mall. At *least* that important.

"Wouldn't it be wonderful if what we *really* believed, if what we *really* felt, we could *tell* each other? And wouldn't it be wonderful if the rest of us would let *them* tell *us*—if they could just be heard? It is our obligation. It is our calling. Whatever it might manifest itself to be within these young adults, however *their* voice comes across, *our* calling to hear and listen remains, even if it does not mirror what we say or reflect—exactly—the way we regard and live our faith.

"Two thousand years of salvation history can certainly withstand what these young men and women have to add with their generation's ideas. Actually, church history beckons their voice because without it, the church would become a museum. Church would not be a boring mediocrity for long, because one of these days it becomes *their* church. They will not have to loiter much longer in the narthex, denied access by aging Gatekeepers.

"The road to Emmaus ends when the two of us, the Unseen Children's Church and the denominational churches, are having dinner with this stranger whom we do not recognize as Jesus. But as He breaks bread with us, we know who He is. And when He leaves us, will we say to each other, 'Why didn't we know who He was? Why didn't we recognize Him? Certainly our hearts were on fire!' I know *their* hearts are on fire. I know *they* are on fire, because it is in their crying eyes.

"Carl Sagan is a voice that often rattles the astro-physics community. The Unseen Children's Church has a voice that rattles the church community. Sagan once wrote that 3.6 million years ago in what is now northern Tanzania, a volcano erupted; the resulting cloud of ash covered the surrounding savannas. In 1979, the paleoanthropologist Mary Leakey found footprints in that ash. And 380,000 kilometers away, in a dry, flat plain that we call the Sea of Tranquillity, there is another footprint, left by the first human to walk on the moon. He went on to say that humanity has come far in those 3.6 million years (or even 4.6 billion—or who knows

" Wouldn't it be wonderful if what we *really* believed, if what we *really* felt, we could *tell* each other? **"**

" Two thousand years of salvation history can certainly withstand what these young men and women have to add with their ideas and their generation's ideas. **"**

" The road to Emmaus ends when the two of us, the Unseen Children's Church and the denominational churches, are having dinner with this stranger whom we do not recognize as Jesus. **"**

" ━━━━━━━━━━━━━━━
Please let them speak for this church.

"The Unseen Children's Church is comprised of high flyers as well as at-risk kids, who are in the majority of teen America. It also encompasses the racially segregated and ignored. Its members are those who have found communion with God **and** denouncing of God outside the mainline denominations, if anywhere."

how many billion years). And we are the conscious conscience of it all. We are the ones who speak for planet Earth. Members of the Unseen Children's Church are the ones who speak for their generation. They speak for this church. Please, let them speak *to* this church and *for* this church before they comprise its Body.

"Eddie Vedder of Pearl Jam has a prophetic word for his generation when he sings, 'Is something wrong? Of course there is…You're still alive…but do I deserve to be? Is that the question? If so, who answers? Who will answer?

"Children, claim access. Finesse it. Storm it. Endear it, until access becomes yours. Demand that your chorus be heard while you seek what you're looking for. That's okay.

"'The Unseen Children's Church,' is a pseudonym. This unseen church is comprised of high flyers as well as at-risk kids, who are in the majority of teen America. It also encompasses the racially segregated and ignored. The Unseen Children's Church members are those who have found communion with God or they denounce God outside the mainline denominations, if anywhere.

"Is that OKAY?"

As the speaker moved from the pulpit, the philharmonic-size African-American multicultural choir filled the building with their rendition of Martin Luther's "A Mighty Fortress Is Our God."

There in the back…far in the back…almost in the narthex, he saw her again.

"Martin, this one is for Sara," he said and he began to sing.

 **HOSPITAL ZONE**

Culture Zone: If your spirit is wounded, take it to the right hospital.

SUNDAY IN THE BIG EASY
...DO YOU REMEMBER THE DAY?

(And the sign said: Everybody welcome to come in today.)

Escorted by Charity and Mercury (you remember him, don'cha?), Sara disembarks the Delta Queen riverboat into the fog of New Orleans' French Quarter. They search for voices in the fog. Sounds of daylight. The travelers climb aboard a trolley and ask, "Can you take us to the place where people Remember the Day?"

From cathedral to fortress and back to the damp Quarter they ride. Hymn-sounds of the faithful fresh in their ears still leave empty hearts. Turning to her companions, Sara says,

> *"There are so many familiar sounds,*
> *Even as many familiar faces and ideas.*
> *But today doesn't seem to be any different from another.*
> *Maybe we don't Remember the Day,*
> *Because we never knew it."*

— *The Ballad of Sara Doom*

On her way to yet another train Sara smiles, "But, I think we'd like to."

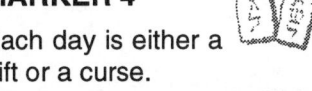

MARKER 4

Each day is either a gift or a curse.
Whichever you choose will determine how you remember it.

> Hymn-sounds of the faithful fresh in their ears still leave empty hearts.

 NO TIME-OUT ZONE

Culture Zone: Too much information with no application.

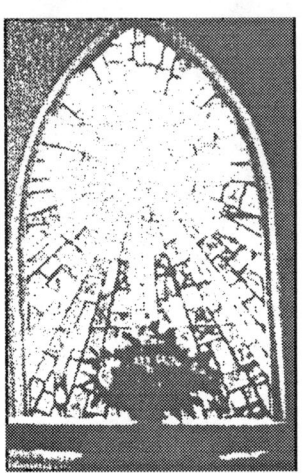

Take us to the place

where people Remember...

the Day...

Hymn sounds of Faith...

"DEAR DAD…"

Hizzoner-the-Mayor was pumping The Writer's hand vigorously. He handed him the Key to the City and flashed his Cheshire Cat grin to the local media.

"Citizens of San Antonio, Texas. It is our honor to present this Key to the City to our own homebody (ha-ha) and welcome him on this historic occasion…"

Hizzoner-the-Mayor went on like this for a short time. The Writer wondered why he let himself be roped into this one. Oh, yes, he remembered… pay the bills…mouths to feed, etc. The River Walk was so San Antonio, he thought, but why do I hear Caribbean tin drum music? Hizzoner-the-Mayor was taking time to kibbitz with the on-air talent, so The Writer glanced toward the drum sound.

There he was—Bongo Jo—happily playing for a few tourists just outside O'Malley's Irish Pub. The Writer remembered…so many times he would find his Dad there, late into the night. So many times Dad would be singing with his cronies till the pub's closing time. So many times he had to take him home despite his father's relentless and colorful Irish protests.

So many times he had to take him home amidst the colorful Irish protests of his father.

Photo Opportunity time was over and his Hizzoner-the-Mayor was glad-handing the crowd. The Writer walked toward Bongo Jo and smiled. His Dad may have exasperated him, even embarrassed him, but he missed him. Bongo Jo winked at The Writer. He remembered. Guess I look a lot like Dad, The Writer thought…hope it honors him. And he embraced Bongo Jo.

BONGO ZONE

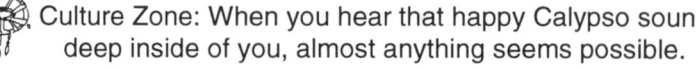

Culture Zone: When you hear that happy Calypso sound deep inside of you, almost anything seems possible.

"THE NAZARETH PROJECT"

...WHAT IS HONOR?
("R-E-S-P-E-C-T...
FIND OUT WHAT IT MEANS TO ME.")

Over and over again, Sara and her companions tried to comprehend their teleporting from one venue to another. Mercury had always been certain the white man's whiskey was to blame for just about everything imaginable, from housing projects to reverse discrimination. (More on that theory, later). And poor little Charity didn't know that the French Quarter's fog wasn't just next door to the River Walk in San Antonio. But Sara knew. At least she knew that the Spirit Father understood a quantum Leap of Faith could (and would) take you anywhere...even places you did not intend to go.

One such leap just occurred. There they stood in the deep night, walking again from there to here. This time along the manicured banks of the San Antonio River's Paseo del Rio. Unwelcome as they were amidst the revelry of convention goers, sightseers, and inevitable party-hardy crowds, our quantum-leapers questioned a friendly looking man in full Mexican cowboy regalia.

"Qué pasa, mí amigo?"

"What's he saying?" Sara asked.

At which Mercury eased into the conversation, "He means, what's goin' down, my friend?"

> **MARKER 5**
> You are a source of credit to your family—good or bad—and the respect you need will be equal to that you give.

> **"**
> But Sara knew. At least she knew that the Spirit Father understood a quantum Leap of Faith could (and would) take you anywhere.... Even places you did not intend to go.
> **"**

Paseo del Rio

Inside a great sadness

The sound of hunger

48

Amused by these three (obviously out-of-place) quantum-leapers, the Tall Cowboy replied quietly, "It's okay. I'm just part of the show for the gringos. It's obvious you three will find no honor among these thieves. I'll direct you in the right direction if you'll tell me *where* it is you are looking for."

"I've lost my ethic, sir, and I don't know *where* to look."

"Well, at least you're looking for it. See all these people? Not only do they *not* know they've lost it...they wouldn't know an ethic if it came up and bit them on the *cascarones*."

At that moment, tourists surrounded the handsome Tall Cowboy, insisting upon grotesque photo opportunities with an authentic South-of-the-Border type. With flash bulb residue still stinging her eyes, Sara cried, "That was so disrespectful."

"It pays the rent, Señorita. Come, I'll show you the way out of here."

Before long our travelers found themselves inside a great sadness. Both barrio and slum it was. Hopelessness hung upon their shoulders like prayer shawls. There were people there, but few moved. Dogs were barking somewhere in the surrounding distance. It was the sound of hunger. Periodically there was the unmistakable pounding of gunfire. From the night a voice spoke, "Welcome to the Nazareth Project."

"Welcome home."

And they skipped into the Christmas Cafe.

It was only a quantum leap away.

 **POVERTY ZONE**

Culture Zone: The place where the poor in spirit should gather to feed the hungry.

"STARSTORM" AT THE CHRISTMAS CAFE

Christmas seems all but forgotten. It has become a money-changers' commotion. Close to midnight on Christmas Eve in a very large metropolis, many people and events converge on The Christmas Cafe.

The Christmas Cafe is in a run-down building. A young pastor gives shelter and food to runaways and society's castaways. His ministry is funded by running The Cafe, where hot music and warm food are served.

Next door is old St. Hillarian's Cathedral. Late on this Christmas Eve, a small band of folks are desperately practicing what might be their final Christmas pageant. The Bishop has charged old Father O'Magolly and the Church Lady, Mrs. Blatzfoom, to come up with a "world-class" pageant—although no one may come to see it.

All these souls are looking for The Miracle that will change their lives. Events begin with a STARSTORM that generates the evening's magic. (A STARSTORM is a cosmic convergence of light and power and awe and wonder and hope.)

STARSTORM

Take me to a place
Where it might begin,
To find some ray of hope
Where there's no place to hide.

A world of death and darkness
Piercing, blinding light,
who will take the hands
Of runaways in the night?

It might take a Starstorm
To get to the light.
It might take a Starstorm,
A Starstorm tonight.

Children without wonder,
Mothers without milk,
Violence, chilling cries,
Clinging to our lives.

Come and hear the Angel
At the Christmas Cafe,
Do not look for heroes,
They have lost their way.

Please believe it's coming,
(Coming) beyond the thunder,
He's coming in a Starstorm
(No) Perfect ending…
(Just Awesome wonder.)

Poor Sara. Quantum Faith Leaping can be very tiring (and confusing). Without notice, one might find oneself on the stage of the Christmas Cafe…singing, "Do not look for heroes…"

— *The Ballad of Sara Doom*
© Michael O. Harrington, 1993

 **STAR ZONE**

 Culture Zone: No, not Elvis and Madonna. You know, the *big* star…a place where it might begin.

"

A Starstorm is a cosmic convergence of light and power and awe and wonder and hope.

"

50

WHATEVER IS NOBLE,
THINK ON THESE THINGS

"Nearer to the face of God than any place on earth,

that is where I want to be," he said.

The Writer stood near the canyon and saw the evening star and her two sisters pulsing in the shivering night sky.

> **"**
> Below them in the canyon, they could see faces in the walls.
>
> Now those faces in the stones screamed...

He, his wife, his sister and brother-in-law had driven back through the forest primeval on their way from there to here. Below them in the canyon, they could see faces in the walls. Now those faces in the stones screamed...

motionless but alive...

they heard their sorrowful litany.

"A thousand thousand Chieftains,
Stone Prince and Princess have died.
Nobility,
Noble...Noble...and Alive."

He closed his eyes when he saw the contrails of more jets arcing through the night's endless dome.

"Headed for L.A.," he said.

"No doubt," his sister agreed.

Had they lingered a moment longer, they might have heard a response lofting from the opposite canyon wall.

"Bring thousands of millions of children,
Lead them here at any cost...
They will see what is worth preserving,
and discover why they are lost."

—*The Ballad of Sara Doom*

CRATER ZONE

Culture Zone: When you are cratering and falling into that great hole of loneliness, listen to the echoes of others on the way down.

THE KILLING OF EAGLES...

WHAT KILLS?

Leaving Mercury and Charity behind in the Nazareth Project was difficult, but necessary. Sara already missed them. But she knew that Charity might not be welcomed where she was going, and Mercury could be her messenger no more. Sara needed a moment with her people. She was nearing the barren reservation now. The rocks were speaking to her again.

> *"O Spirit Father...where are the eagles?*
> *I need their wings...I fear* ♪ ♫
> *my ethic may not be lost,*
> *But it may be simply dead."*
>
> — *The Ballad of Sara Doom*

A mountain of stones moved. The cracking of rocks split the chilly night air. Thunder without light exploded in the distance.

"They're killing the eagles again," roared the Stone Master looking over the valley beyond. Then he turned his gaze upon Sara. "You may be too late, Princess. The eagles are seeking shelter under the cloak of darkness, and the evil ones are returning from the hunt."

Sara bowed before the Stone Master, weeping. "I've seen a great ugliness on my journey, Master of Stone. Peoples' actions hold great danger for creatures of the Spirit Father."

"Peoples' *words* are just as deadly. Come. Listen to the voices echoing from the victims' canyon."

Sara took the great warrior's hand. He led her to the edge of a great crevice in the earth hewn by hatred, by ten thousand of thousands of years of human cruelty. The silence of the sand of screams threw Sara to her knees. Into the warrior's eyes she searched for some small measure of relief. He smiled.

> *"Princess, if not for your lust for hope,* ♪ ♫
> *We would be extinct.*
> *Because you continue your endless journey,*
>   *we have courage,*
>   *and since you believe without proof that night*
>   *must some way give into the day...*
> *It will be so."*
>
> — *The Ballad of Sara Doom*

MARKER 6
Extreme prejudice is just that...deadly.
If you can't keep your mouth shut, then let's talk.

"

Sara took the great warrior's hand. He led her to the edge of a great crevice in the earth hewn by the hatred of ten thousand of thousands of years of human cruelty.

"

"Earthquakes, fires, and riots, Oh my!"

ME-TV ZONE

Culture Zone: That sneaking suspicion that you are on some really bad reality TV show without a laugh track.

"Is my destination far, Master of Stone?"

"It is perilous, Princess."

"Then I must go while there is still an eagle alive."

> "The Stone Master is the Creator;
>
> The Stone Warrior is the Protector of Creation"

 **WAR ZONE**

Culture Zone: Not merely a place of conflict but a place to take a stand.

 *VIEW FROM A CONVERTIBLE RABBIT*

Trying to escape yet another L.A. traffic jam, The Writer's sister turned onto Sunset Strip heading for Laurel Canyon Drive. Sitting in the back seat, the view from the convertible Rabbit takes on the feel of being a trailing float in the Rose Bowl Parade (just after the horses). Towering over the Strip, Geraldo Rivera's mustached smile glared at him with 20-foot letters, asking, "Cannibalistic surf-Nazi housewives are coming to L.A. Think anyone will notice?"

It was directly beside the billboard that read, "Earthquakes, fires, and riots, Oh my!"

Soon they turned toward U.C.L.A.'s garland-encrusted campus, past the sign that proclaimed, "Like any decent place, advance reservations are advised. Mt. Sinai Mortuary."

After endless avenues of Beverly Hills' perfectly planted rows of coordinated tree-lined mansions, they cruised Rodeo Drive only to stop beside the Beverly Hills Presbyterian Church. The placard proclaimed, *"Sunday's Sermon: Appearance and Reality—The Rev. Jim Morrison."*

The Writer began to laugh uncontrollably as the Rabbit turned onto Laurel Canyon Road. Even in the dead of summer, the air was crisp. Looking at the skeleton of what was once Jim Morrison's house (circa 1960s), he wondered, "Can Sara ever forgive us? I wonder."

SUNSET STRIP
DON'T DEHUMANIZE!
("I'M JUST A MATERIAL GIRL...")

The Creature was cross-dressed between a court jester and a leather sales-man. Jingling—tingling—and spiking its way down the strip, the fool approached. Sashaying up to Sara, The Creature spoke. "Whatcha gotta sell? Whatcha gonna buy? Gimme some...Whatcha want?...Can ya spare a dime?"

Sara gasped, "I...I've lost my ethic, and I don't know where...Oh never mind."

The Creature squealed in demonic delight. Calling other night crawlers around, it laughed. "Another tiny toon, brothers and sisters!"

They began to close in on Sara. Just then the crowd parted like a Cecil B. DeMille out-take. A muscular pint-sized woman appeared in their midst. She rocked this way, and they swooned. She rocked that way, and they wailed. In the hush, someone blurted, "My god! It's Madonna!"

The gaggle of weirdoes fell on their faces, sore afraid. Then the Mother of your mother's worst nightmares spoke. "Ain't nothin' quite as scary as seein' what can't be believed, is it, honey? Now, back off, you cheese balls and make room for a real time traveler. C'mon fresh face, I'll show ya the town."

And off they went into the sparkling underbelly of 20th-Century foxiness. You see, it takes a black rose to make a mountain laurel smell so sweet—and seem so very far away. Odd as it may seem, Sara felt more at ease with Madonna than she would have ever suspected. Maybe it was because she was so suspect herself. In a dehumanized society, it can take the outrageous to pin-point something so pure. Sara could still hear Grandfather's voice in faces of the homeless. Even on Sunset Strip.

> **MARKER 7**
> You will never be so grateful as when someone rescues you from your own culture.

"

In a dehumanized society, it can take the outrageous to pinpoint something pure.

54

"Remember, Princess...
Whatever is pure...
Whatever is beautiful...
Whatever holds the good vision...
Think about these things."

— *The Ballad of Sara Doom*

"You hearin' voices, honey?" the Mother of your mother's worst nightmares wanted to know.

OZONE

Culture Zone: Sometimes people and situations seem just so bizarre that they draw us in.

"SLIP SLIDING AWAY...FROM L.A."

On Route 101 Ventura Freeway, American-made cars seem outnumbered ten to one. They are five lanes deep in both directions. People. Cars. People in every car under the sun, tailpipe to radiator. People shaving—reading—cellular phoning—lap tops—faxes—headaches—bottled water sipping—make-up—almost every vehicle with one person. Loneliness spawns up river in a flood of soloists. No one seems to notice...no one. The cars look like pock-marked faces, uncaring. The "Looky Loos" are slowing down the traffic, again. A relentless exodus from there to here. It is mindless, passive and meaningless non-motion, massaged by the futility of it all. Caught in a 10-MPH ooze with a hundred thousand other captives of the endless blacktop ballet, The Writer looks for signs of life. All the while Paul Simon is crooning on the radio, "The nearer your destination, the more you're slip-sliding away."

And the obnoxious effluvia of a billion ozone-eating bacteria from the miracle of internal combustion busily choke the last vestige of humanity from our brains. Rising in an inexorable assent of poison from the desert floor, it forms a wavy mirage in the sub-cosmic heat.

And the mirage looked like heaven.

"A relentless exodus from there to here.

The mirage looked like money.

It was not there.

OUTTA-HERE ZONE

Culture Zone: This is too much...bye, bye...I'm history...I'm outta-here.

BY THE GLOW OF BURNING BUILDINGS' LIGHT...

WHAT DID YOU STEAL?
(A DAY IN THE NIGHT OF SOUTH CENTRAL L.A.)

Following directions from the homeless can be more promising than it might seem. Since they go unnoticed, slipping in where angels fear to tread becomes second nature. All Sara knew was that she needed to look for the amber glow of burning buildings' light. Sure enough...there they were...pulsing in the night.

There were guards posted. Through the flames, their shadows danced, more foreboding than Beefeaters at the Tower of London. Sara was able to smile.

"Pardon me, but I think I must pass through this place." No answer came from beyond his dark sunglasses. "Please sir. I'm supposed to see a Mr....Big Al."

> *The flames from the burning buildings stopped.*
> *The screaming of the children stopped.*
> *The police sirens stopped.*
> *Even the automatic gunfire stopped.*
> *Everything just stopped.*
> — *The Ballad of Sara Doom*

From behind the guards, a man the size of Stone Warrior approached. "Welcome to Watts" was all he said.

Into the nether world of contemporary terror they walked.

"But the flames, where did they go?" Big Al's laugh filled the empty streets. "It's controlled with gas jets. Keeps up the right appearance. Suburbia expects it."

"And the screaming and..."

"Gunfire? Sirens? Hey, Hey...CD ROM recordings. State-of-the-art terrorizing. Whole thing's a show. Can't have a perpetual riot without diddling with technology. For Mary and Joseph's sake, it's too exhausting to do the real thing."

"Then it's a fake. All the violence isn't real?"

MARKER 8

If they take away your home... you're homeless. If they take away your heart... you're helpless.

"
Into the nether world of contemporary terror they walked.

"Oh, it's *real* enough honey. But most folks thinks stealin' and riotin' and the like looks like this. The *real* thing is much too complex for most folks to understand."

"Don't you want them to understand, Mr. Big Al?"

"If they did, they'd only take more of what we ain't got."

Sara sat down on a street corner and shook her head. Big Al looked at her and knelt down. "Ever see Arsenio Hall, little one? No? Well he don't get it either. C'mon, I'll show you."

 **FIRE ZONE**

Culture Zone: The feeling that the urban landscape is a tinder box just waiting for a match.

Sorrowfully, Sara clutched her flower as she stood in front of the gutted 7-Eleven in Watts and said "Then it's a fake."

WHY THE J. PAUL GETTY MUSEUM HIDES ABOVE MALIBU

On Malibu Beach, red rocks jut like rusted sentinels of Manifest Destiny searching the Pacific Westward for one more moment of glorious conquests.

The J. Paul Getty Museum is a recreation of a first-century A.D. Roman country villa, complete with interior and exterior gardens. Nestled high above the Pacific Coast Highway in Malibu, between Sunset and Topanga Canyon Boulevards, the museum languishes in quiet, tranquil civility. Its collection of Roman and Greek antiquities, spanning 3000 B.C. to early A.D., boasts classic Grecian urns, a marble Aphrodite, cyclamate clay figures, and the curious Kouros mystery. Along with all that, there are works by Rembrandt, Rubens, Renoir, Van Gogh, drawings…and illuminated Byzantine and French manuscripts. Even has some Napoleonic gilded-gold-silver-decorative-nobility objects of wanton wealth, forged from the blood of peasant multitudes.

Stand in the herb garden amidst the fragrance of woolly thyme, common toad flax and rupture wort: The voices of children are missing.

Stand in the herb garden amidst the fragrance of woolly thyme, common toad flax and rupture wort: The voices of children are missing. This stuff should be their passion, their inheritance, their home.

Far below on the coastline is Malibu…

Far above, the J. Paul Getty trembles behind wolly thyme…

 **CIVILITY ZONE**

Culture Zone: Lovely moments when you find yourself held in the trembling hands of ancient civilization's innocence and when classical "Artsy" Stuff actually looks cool.

THE BEACH BOYS.
THANK THEM FOR THE OCEAN

Malibu: Where bungalows and condos huddle so close together they look like stubby children holding hands, ready to jump into the ocean below.

Beach front property…with no beach.

Malibu, home of surfers (without a wave), Alice's Restaurant (with no Arlo), fishermen (without a catch), the famous (without a clue), and Mudslide Slim (without a tune).

58

And on they went
In a birdless brown sky.
Does anyone look up
Or ever ask why?

Next stop—Nevada.

Onward to Topanga Canyon
Where aging Hippies thrive.
And the faces in the rocks
observe migrations
to the sea…
to Malibu.

— *The Ballad of Sara Doom*

NO SWIMMING ZONE

Culture Zone: The feeling that it's not the ocean that's toxic.

While the Pacific Coast Highway crawls beside towering clay mountains, Pepperdine University gawks in insolent indifference, its backsides mooning the mainland, and its dazed face expressionless…like a lighthouse without a beacon.

The chilly wind is out of place here.
The obscene opulence of its homes are monuments to excess.
It should be hot here (but it's chilly).
It should be blazing hot.
Hot with shame.

The Writer rubbed his burning eyes. He squinted and looked down the dangerous coastline, from Malibu to L.A. Down that expanse of infamous beach was South Central. Somewhere out there was Watts. It was burning. Always burning. He shook his head and prayed,

"Father…be with your child Sara tonight.
At least one more night."

The Writer turned and began to descend the mountain to the gray sand far far below.

And to the Beach Boys…

Thank them for the Ocean…

"East coast girls may be hip, Midwest farmers' daughters may make you feel alright… but Vegas girls bring the ocean to the desert…but I wish they all could be California girls…"

BACK LOTS AND BACKDROPS
TABLOID REALITY
(THE PHANTOM OF STUDIO CITY)

Big Al carried Sara to the threshold of tinsel town, Studio City. This is the place where reality takes a right turn into celluloid sickness. News bytes, sound bytes, and positive spins have nothing on this place. Where the industry once could transport us from Tara to Iwo Jima to Casablanca and back again, back lots of Hollywood now perform exorcisms on our overloaded minds and strain our spirits through the popcorn notion of what most 13 year olds would assess as "COOL!"

As Big Al promised, they stopped by the resurrected "Arsenio Hall Show." Although the audience's rhythmic "Uh-Uh-Uh" was refreshing, it resembled a tribal ritual of sorts. And while it was kind of like the "Letterman Show," everyone—host, guests, musicians and audience—flirted with anger. All the while, the host taunted, "Let's Get Busy!"

"Why do they seem so upset, Big Al?" Sara wanted to know as they left.

"Truth is...they don't know what the truth is."

"Will they ever?"

"Not as long as sellin' Coca-Cola is more important than feedin' hungry babies."

In the greenroom of another tabloid reality talk show, waiting among Mothers Who Date Their Ex-Husband's Children and some trailer park people protesting mandatory public education, Big Al handed Sara over to an old war buddy. Strider really was a piece of work. After three tours in 'Nam skipping choppers from one hole to another, he was now engaged in part-time stunt work and island hopping for the idle rich. Many hand rituals and hugs later, Big Al made the intros.

"Strider, this here quarter-sized drink o'water is Sara Doom...She's in between there and here, and she needs a lift."

Strider scratched his graying mustache and lifted his mirrored sunglasses. "Weren't you in that teenage disaster movie with Shannen Doherty and Ice T 'bout the life of Janis Joplin and Jimi Hendrix?"

"No sir, Mr. Strider. I've lost my ethic and I need an eagle to fly me where I can find it."

The two war vets exchanged glances.

> **MARKER 9**
> In the search for truth, don't buy someone else's reality. It rarely fits.

> " Truth is...they don't know what the truth is.   —Big Al "

"Let's get busy."

"Well, Big Al, I gotta twin engine on the back lot that ain't doin' much. But, I'm a little short on cash."

Big Al handed him a small roll of bills. "Go parlay this into some travlin' money. It's a long flight from there to here to find an excellent thing."

"Vegas?"

"Vegas."

"Okay, big'un, I got one more shot on this film and I'll be ready. Gotta drop Stallone and Schwartzenegger into some blazing Zen Temples so they can blow up half of Mainland China."

Strider jumped into his chopper with the two mega-stars (and their stunt men). Big Al knelt down beside Sara. "Sweetheart, please remember this: People gonna tell you all manner of crap just to get the upper hand on ya. Keep lookin' in their eyes, tho'...cause you'll either see the fire burnin' like Watts, or an empty tomb."

"I think this is the beginning of a beautiful friendship."

They strolled into fog machine smoke curling around their feet on the fake tarmac of 20th-Century's back lot.

"
Gotta drop Stallone and Schwartzenegger into some blazing Zen Temples so they can blow up half of Mainland China. — Strider
"

 BOZO ZONE (*AKA*: BOZONE)

Culture Zone: What's the difference between Bozo the Clown and a TV talk show host? Oh, about 1.3 million a year. Just listening to them sends you to the BOZONE.

FACELESS ROCKS...ARE JUST ROCKS

Fleeing from L.A. can be traumatic for the novice escapee. The terrain changes so rapidly and the elevations so dramatically that the traveler experiences sensory overload and a heavy dose of culture *schlock*.

From Studio City northeast on I-5 flows another endless motionless river of cars. You drive past Ventura and Laurel Canyon, into the San Bernadino foothills and through the "Flintstones" movie on-location site. The climb away from L.A. is constant. But at least it's away from L.A.

A Jim Morrison wanna-be along with his Meg Ryan look-a-like sat beneath towering rocks on the sand floor. Long hair flapping in the hot winds, shirtless he climbed onto one of the sentinels. Pointing a silly finger below him he shouted, "Hey lookit...they're shootin' some kinda movie or something."

And sure enough, they were shooting some kind of movie (or something) right there, cradled between sheer rock and violent sea. The ocean is more dangerous here, more alive, muscular. It was an MTV-90s-western-sitcom-pilot-wanna-be...30 or so 20-Somethings (bodies all ripe with the glow of microwaved chicken) were pampering their priceless equipment.

> And sure enough, they were shooting some kind of movie (or something) right there cradled between sheer rock and violent sea.

Looking at his wife and sister, The Writer wanted to ask, "Why in God's name does anybody put up with this?" But he remembered why. He couldn't escape The Why. No one could. So he smiled. "I sure wanted to see a baby seal."

"Sorry, Bubba," his sister said.

Four fat sea gulls had been observing them. Suddenly they padded proudly forward as if to say, "We know we're not some adorable little endangered seal cub...but will we do?"

Past faceless rocks they rode, away from L.A.

 **FALLING-ROCK ZONE**

Culture Zone: The danger of a Falling Rock Zone is that one of them is bound to have your name on it.

WHY, IF TRIGGER WEREN'T STUFFED, I'D RIDE 'EM RIGHT INTO VEGAS, SHOOT UP THE PLACE AN' MAKE EVERYBODY DO RIGHT— BUT FIRST, I'D LIKE SOME REAL COOL SEQUINED BOOTS, AND...

> **"**
>
> He did not smile. He just drove from there to here, and mumbled, "There is no excellent thing."
>
> **"**

"Finally!" The Writer exclaimed. "Out of L.A. I never *ever* want to go back to that over-inflated greed pool."

"Right, so we're going to Las Vegas for some *culture*," remarked his wife.

He did not smile. He just drove from there to here, and he mumbled, "There *is* no excellent thing."

Sunset on the Sierra Madras came with a violent gush of colors. A jet floated above them with contrails hurling to LAX. It is silent up here. No faces in the rocks. A moonscape below rocky cathedrals guards nothing. They are silent faceless giants without a name—watchers in the night.

They drove past Palmdale, home to NASA shuttle landings, and chée-chée tract housing in the Adobe Desert. They drove through the barren forest of Joshua trees as they came alive at night, only to freeze into their curious crookedness at dawn.

They drove past Barstow, home of the Roy Rogers and Dale Evans museum.

...Past the signs, "This Way Vegas," "That Way Needles," "Route 66" and past "Rosalie's Good Eats Cafe."

The convertible Rabbit whizzed down Route 66, and he swore he saw Troy Donahue riding Trigger.

ROUTE 66 SPEED ZONE

Culture Zone: That feeling like you are in a 60s black and white TV drama series endlessly slowing down in hopes of running across your culture.

DUEL AT CAESAR'S PALACE...

WHOSE STUFF DO YOU WANT...ANYWAY.
(YOU'VE GOT GREAT STUFF!)

Strider's twin engines roared heavily as he smacked the flying carcass down on a Vegas runway. "Eagle's Wings" was still belching smoke and the chorus of an old Beatles tune as they deplaned (or bailed out, the way Sara saw it). "But the fool on the hill sees the sun going down..." Lennon sang on.

"Look, Sara, I gotta take this cash and try to get us some flyin' money. I'll drop you on the Strip for some sightseein', then meet you back here in two hours."

Sara Doom stood, stunned, on the main drag of Las Vegas. It had been so long since she had seen daylight that the fifty billion candlepower display of human indignity quaking before her eyes was nearly more than she could bear. Rippling lights formed the outlines of naked women dancing in primitive synchronization with vulgar shapes of human excess. Greed seeped from the pores of every image like wax dripping from a monstrous replica of Sodom after God cleaned house.

All Sara could think was that the burning of Watts could not have been this awful. Oh, the weird characters she saw on *this* street!

Each one wanting the others' stuff. Everyone wanting more and more stuff. Whirling one-armed bandits of our time assembled like an army of garish gunslingers. Zombies promising life. Then, standing next to someone covered in tiny mirrors, Strider spoke to Sara. "Sara.. Sara! Wake up."

"Have I been dreaming, Strider? Please tell me so."

"Sorry, no...but we are in luck, if you believe in such magic."

Sara shook her head. "You didn't gamble, did you?"

MARKER 10
There is one God. 
There is one You.
Get to know you, too.

"

Sara Doom stood in shock on the main drag of Las Vegas. It had been so long since she had seen daylight that the fifty billion candlepower display of human indignity quaking before her eyes was nearly more than she could bear.

"

"How should I know. I'm just the pilot. You're the one lookin' for some lost relic..."

"*Ethic*," she interrupted.

Strider removed his mirrored shades and rubbed his red-white-blue eyes. "Yeah...I lost, but don't worry. Here's the deal. My friend, Wayne, is takin' some business associates to Norway for the Winter Olympics. Doncha get it? He's hired us to take 'im."

"*US?*"

"Just follow my lead and we'll be there."

"Where is *there*?"

"How should I know. I'm just the pilot. You're the one lookin' for some lost relic..."

"Ethic," she interrupted.

"Whatever. Anyway, I don't know much about Norway but anybody who's anybody is gonna be there. Certainly someone can help you find your ethic. Besides, it ain't *here*."

Thinking back to Wally Skydancer, Sara mused, "That's the problem, isn't it? Not only do we *not* know the right stuff and want everybody else's stuff...we don't even know our own stuff. Take us to Norway, Strider."

"Don't bet on the human spirit, Sara," he said. "At least not in Vegas without an inside straight."

(Thus endeth Part Two of *The Ballad of Sara Doom*)

 **TAKE-OFF ZONE**

Culture Zone: It's like when you feel you've got all the right stuff you need, but you ache to find some other stuff. So you just take off.

I MEAN SYNCOPATED ELECTRIC LIGHT SHOW ANIMATION IT MAY BE, BUT IT AIN'T NO HOOVER DAM.

"Hoover Dam was built to hold back the Colorado River's flooding and to develop electrical power. Near the Depression's end, 7,000 people were hauled up here to build an entire city. They worked around the clock using enough concrete to build a highway from one side of the United States to the other." The old tour guide took a breath and another dip of snuff. "Each side of this gorge has two 30-foot-tall tunnels built to reroute the river during construction of the dam. After completion, it made the world's largest man-made lake, Lake Mead." He moved closer to the edge and everyone looked down the dam's sheer, massive wall. "The water is over 600 feet deep on the other side of this dam," he said and moved on.

People moved quietly past The Writer. People are polite and kind up here, he thought. People are in awe.

And then there's Vegas......

The MGM Grand is the largest hotel on earth, with over 8,000 rooms and 7800 full-time employees. It took over half a billion dollars to build it. Inside is a theme park, MGM Grand Adventure. Everyone greets you with a, "Hope you have a Grand day."

Other than that, they are incredibly rude.

There is the MGM Garden with its 15,000- seat arena for prize fights and the like. And, of course, there are the Casino, 11 restaurants, and the shopping mall. It is all green—emerald green—even the glass is emerald green. There is a complete reproduction of the Emerald City of Oz with a sky seven stories high where there are day and night and thunderstorms and stars and the movie's Hot Air Balloon (Wizard On Board). And there are the Yellow Brick Road, Dorothy, Toto, the Tin Man, Cowardly Lion, and Scarecrow. The trees even talk to you. So you move out the main entrance through a huge lion's mouth...

Across the street is the Excalibur. It is a castle with jousting knights and jugglers and Elaine Boozler saying, "Las Vegas is Nevada for buffet." Video arcades and slot machines, blackjack and slot machines, virtual reality and more slot machines.

Down the street is the Luxor—a solid black glass pyramid with a larger-than-Sphinx Sphinx. It has the most powerful light beam on the face of this planet shooting straight up in the sky, (you can see it in L.A.). You could read a newspaper ten miles above it...(if you take the time). Wait-

> People are polite to us here. People are in awe.

AND THEN......

> Everyone greets you, "Hope you have a Grand day."

Other than that, they are incredibly rude.

...and make elephants disappear and have a white tiger that is extinct in the wild, but they are raising them and make them disappear. Roy rides a white stallion, and they both disappear. And they fly around, and disappear.

ing inside are the River Nile barge rides, Archeological Tour, a museum about King Tut's history (with complete replicas). And, in front: At night a water screen comes to life with holograms…

An even *bigger* complex is under construction. Buildings for blocks were bought and imploded. The Rolling Stones held a sell-out concert on the flat property. It will boast two complete floating casinos.

And don't forget Caesar's Palace Mall forum shops, a ceiling with sunrise to sunset at all hours, Saks Fifth Avenue, slots; in the fountain were Baccus (the god of wine) and other statues (twice human size), which (on the hour) talk and move. There's the Mirage, with a volcano erupting every hour. Inside are the two famous magicians, Siegfried and Roy, who live in a Moroccan Palace and make elephants disappear and have a white tiger that is extinct in the wild, but they are raising them and make them disappear. Roy rides a white stallion, and they both disappear. And they fly around, and disappear. At Treasure Island there are two full-size ships, and every 90 minutes the full-scale pirate ship floats around the moat and sinks the British ship up to its mast—and the heat is so intense you have to turn away from the smoldering lagoon.

All that makes you tick—whatever it is that makes you tick—is forgotten …right there…it is GONE.

People knock you down and don't even say they are sorry. They don't see you anymore. People here have a glassy look. Parents smack kids and shout…

"All you want is more, more, more!
You want what you want, when you
want it. Well shut up! Life's tough!"

Whatever makes you want to be something else.

Nothing, but the best in Vegas.
Nothing but pleasure.
Get the money.
Get more money.
Get money.
Get it?

Las Vegas is nothing like Hoover Dam.

 **DEUCES-ARE-WILD ZONE**

Culture Zone: That unmistakable feeling that your three-of-a-kind will take the pot, but someone's always holding an inside straight.

A DAY IN THE LIFE AT ST. HILLARIAN'S

"YIKES! Quick Miss Blatzfoom...Alert the Altar Guild...hide the sacramental wine...Call the Bishop for Jumpin' Joseph's sake!"

Purebread's the name, gettin' down's my game. We're gonna pop some Hip Hop in your be-bop and kick mediocrity in its "who-who."

PUREBREAD

PART THREE

A CHALLENGE
FOR CHANGE

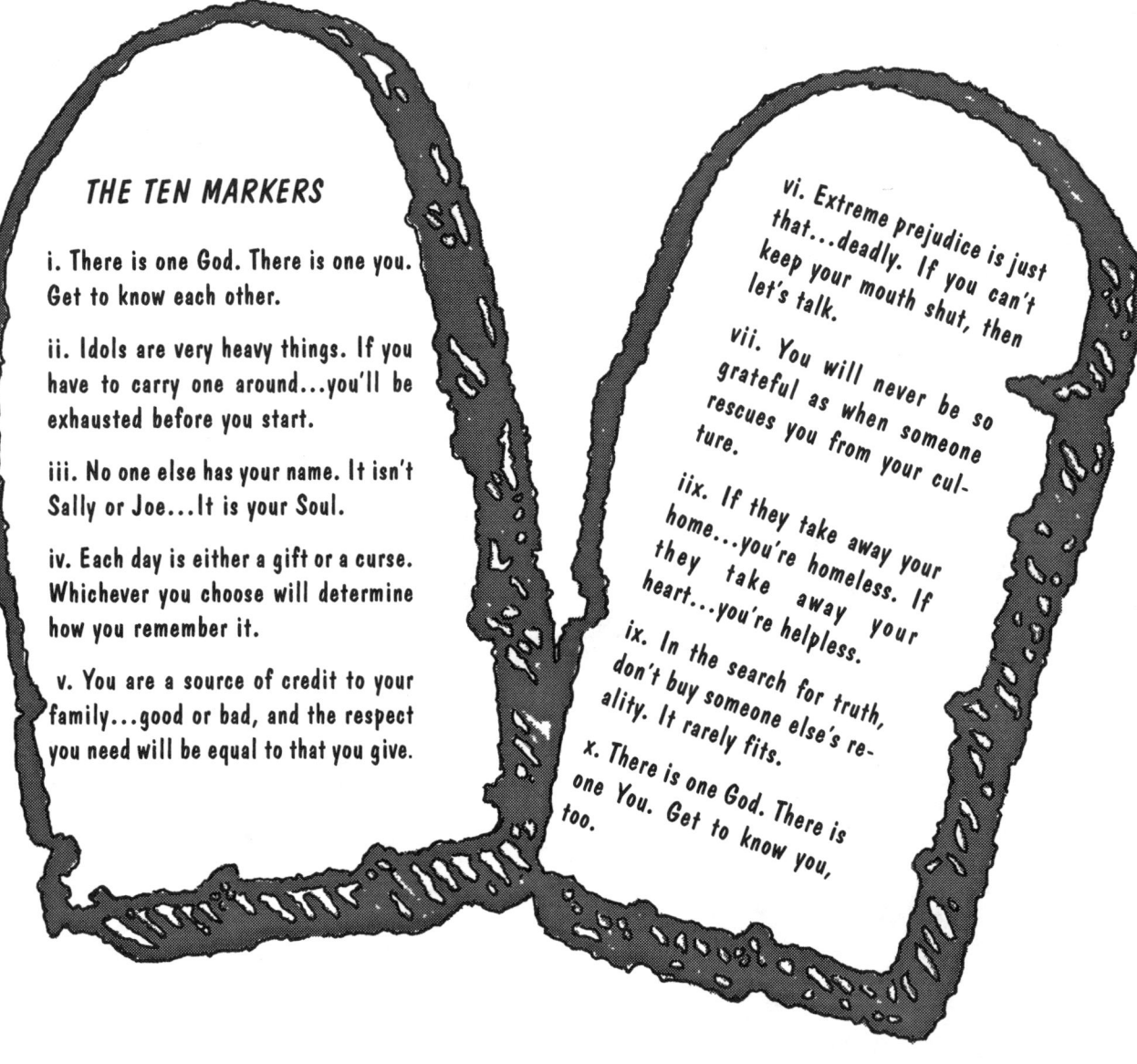

THE TEN MARKERS

i. There is one God. There is one you. Get to know each other.

ii. Idols are very heavy things. If you have to carry one around...you'll be exhausted before you start.

iii. No one else has your name. It isn't Sally or Joe...It is your Soul.

iv. Each day is either a gift or a curse. Whichever you choose will determine how you remember it.

v. You are a source of credit to your family...good or bad, and the respect you need will be equal to that you give.

vi. Extreme prejudice is just that...deadly. If you can't keep your mouth shut, then let's talk.

vii. You will never be so grateful as when someone rescues you from your culture.

iix. If they take away your home...you're homeless. If they take away your heart...you're helpless.

ix. In the search for truth, don't buy someone else's reality. It rarely fits.

x. There is one God. There is one You. Get to know you, too.

...Update...Doom update...Update...There has been an Elvis sighting...Film at Eleven...Update...Doom update...There has been an Elvis sighting...Film

As we speak, some relatively unknown Writer (AKA: a Chronicler of the latter 20th-century's craziness) is seated upon a rented canvas chaise lounge (royal blue, real wood slats) underneath a rented ($12.00 a day) beach-tested umbrella (royal blue—yes, actual wooden pole)...looking out on the amazing blue-aqua-turquoise-royal blue sea off the coast of Florida. J.D. (recent grad of "Ole Miss") has just stopped by to chat on

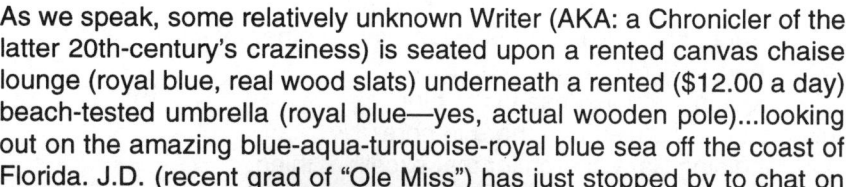

his way to join his casual game of ping. The Writer's ing on the lounge middle-aged three- Scotia takes a break at a passing school Writer looks up from ens of those mag- dance. Three Phan- head on their way to just wiped out on a The sun beats down fusing images with play their game of serenade of cas- appeared now. The briefly with a quick bronzed buddies in a ocean-kayak surf skip- youngest child is snooz- beside him. A post- some of widows from Nova from sun worshipping to gawk of dolphins. The sunburned the papers just in time to view doz- nificent creatures in their timeless tom jets roar a few miles over- God-knows-where. J.D.'s pal has skiffle board in a curling wave... upon the powder-white sand, con- its glare. The three Nova Scotians Velcro ball and mitt catch amid the cading waves...The dolphins have dis- jets have, too. A sandpiper pauses glare at The Writer... as if to say…

"That's the problem with change, isn't it?" And then it ran away. The Writer watched his two-year-old daughter chasing sea gulls in the space between flimsy condos and timeless sea. Looking out past the horizon, his soul cried to the dunes…

"But what of Sara Doom?"

 **DUNE ZONE**

Culture Zone: It takes so much money to keep an Emerald Beach clean, safe and private...so a privileged few can play on the other side of reality on the other side of the dunes.

...Update...Doom update...Update...There has been an Elvis sighting... Film at Eleven... Update... Doom update...There has been an Elvis sighting...Film

"On a Plane From There to Here."

Writing on a jumbo jet is an artificial business.
Writing on a jumbo jet with your desk on your
        lap makes body parts fall asleep.
Writing on a jumbo jet is better than musing
        about armadillos and Blue Devils and other tactical
        personifications of those
        lost in the nonsense of the nineties.
Writing on a jumbo jet from there to here,
        helping Sara search for that excellent thing,
        he is distracted by
A half-naked Demi Moore doing cheesecake with her banker on
        the hyper-glossy cover of *Forbes.*
And *USA Today's* full-four-color-fab-newsie-blurbline-
        Page One-no one-knew this-before-we printed it-
        last-night-interactive-crappola
        "Violence is spreading like wildfire..."
        (subhead: 'I want solutions')

> **"**
> Writing on a jumbo jet from there
> to here, helping Sara search for
> that excellent thing,
> **"**

And the in-flight monitors beaming Steven King's *The Stand*—(apoca-
lyptic-humans-deserve it) and its battle between Good and Satan (a
star-strewn-mega-media-blitzed-super series), with NBA hall-of-famer
Kareem Abdul Jabbar striding the Big Apple's panic-ridden streets
wearing sackcloth and droning—

"The time is now! The Darkman is coming!"

And you wonder, "Excuse me?"

Writing on a jumbo jet,

one prays for the success of *Sara Doom.*

 **SONIC-BOOM ZONE**

Culture Zone: You can move as fast as you want from there to
here, but eventually sound will catch up with you and...BOOM!

CHAPTER 1

ONE COLD NIGHT IN LILLEHAMMER

It was snowing again. Strider had deposited his cargo of Wayne Newton groupies at the Olympic tram, and Sara was alone on a crowded main street of quaint Lillehammer. She would have appreciated the authentic gingerbread house—its other-century ambiance—if she had the time and luxury. But she did not.

All Sara knew at that moment was: It is still snowing, it is still night, she is still alone, she is still hungry, she still doesn't understand the language, and her ethic (or was that "relic") is still as lost as she feels. Suddenly, the crowd surged when a faceless voice screamed, "Look, it's Jack Nicholson!" Sara felt a strong arm pull her out of the cold crowd into the warmth of a local saloon. Looking at her rescuer, Sara smiled, "Thank you, sir. I don't know if I could survive another Elvis sighting." The tall man adjusted his large cowboy hat and let loose a hearty laugh. His long yellow hair fell over the shoulders of a buckskin coat.

"Feelin' a tad outta place, little lady? My name's John Wesley, by way of Kerrville, Texas, skies. This here's my band Hondo. Doin' a little Tex-Mex musical for the international set. Very nuevo-western thing. Ya'll lost or something?"

"Or something. It's my ethic that's lost, Mr. John Wesley,"

"And you actually think you might find an ethic *here*?" The gravelly voice seemed to come from a rather large, gray, armor-plated creature with a long anteater-type snout, a filterless cigarette dangling from its lips.

"Great Sitting Bull's ghost, what is *that*?" Sara asked.

John Wesley hooked his thumbs into his belt, somewhat embarrassed. "Pardon, my friend, ma'am. This here is Hondo. He's a, well, an armadillo. Lets us use his name for the band. He's not what you'd call friendly. A real cynical sort."

"Cynic? You wound me, Tex. Why, I'm positively morose. And wouldn't you be, too, after witnessing two centuries of human de-evolution? But we are being rude. Who is our young traveler?"

> **"**
> My name's John Wesley...Doin' a little Tex-Mex musical for the international set....Very nuevo-western thing. Are ya'll lost or something?

Pardon, my friend, ma'am. This here is Hondo. He's a, well, an armadillo.

"

But this chosen generation has lost its ethic. And the enemy had taken it years past.

"

Sara bowed to the amazing creature. "Sara Doom. At your service, Sir Hondo of the great and honored Armadillo Tribe."

The old 'dillo snickered. "Finally, Johnboy, a prophet. Tell me, young princess, what do you seek?"

"My ethic, sir."

Hondo crushed out his cigarette and eyed the young woman. "Now this should be interesting. How do you know your ethic is lost?"

Sara sat cross-legged before him. Tears welled up in her eyes. "Grandfather told me. I was praying one morning when I felt a tremendous sadness come over the Badlands."

"Badlands?" John Wesley's brow arced.

"Put a sock in it, Johnboy. Can't you see we're in the presence of History? Sheesh, don't you got no manners, son! Continue, please. As a fellow Texan once said, 'I'm all ears.'" With a grin, the old 'dillo twitched each ear.

Sara finally smiled and wiped away her tears. "You see, Mr. John Wesley, the Badlands of Dakota is a place where the medicine is very strong. Grandfather told me the sadness I sensed was a cry of my generation. He said, through many many moons the Great Spirit Father had been waiting for us to stand up."

> *To stand with the creatures of mother earth.*
> *To listen in the wind for the voice within us.*
> *But this chosen generation has lost its ethic.*
> *The enemy had taken it years past.*
> — *The Ballad of Sara Doom*

"Grandfather said I must find our ethic or the sun would not rise one day, and night would stay forever. I brought my medicine: this magic eagle feather, some sage to burn, and this stone from the Badland plain. But we need much medicine to stop the cold and end the night and capture pain. Do you have medicine, honorable Hondo?"

"Possibly. Where has your quest taken you, my child?"

Sara lit a piece of sage. Its purple-gray smoke rose statically. The room disappeared into her voice.

> *"Skydancer sang to the Badlands moon.*
> *Search for your ETHIC...*
>   *in the Ballad of Sara Doom.*
> *In a place of stone the white man calls Chicago*
> *I asked an angry young man for an ABSOLUTE*
> *He had not one to give.*

Off the blast of light from Times Square
a man named Letterman spoke a LANGUAGE
I did not understand.

I wanted the Roundball Dancers to
tell me what is ACCEPTABLE.
They just played their game in the snow.
They did not know.

On a hell-bound train with black Mercury
I rode to meet the Big E.
Between hot cocoa and the unification theory
of what is ETERNAL
I was lost.

And then Mrs. Tipper agreed
and Rev. Jesse said "Amen!"
And there was no VALUE
And I was short changed
*   (or short on change)*

To which Shaq slam-dunked the Mouse
in a dazzling Disney-moment
just to QUALIFY
for who knows what?

Clearing his throat with a shot of Lillehammer moose juice, the old 'dillo shifted his mighty blades. John Wesley and Hondo were on stage wailing away at jet-setting boys and girls.

"Beyond my reach
A lonesome falcon flies.
Within my heart
I still see…
My endless Kerrville skies
Her perfect ice blue eyes."

Hondo lit another cigarette. A glow from his match revealed the anticipation in his ancient eyes. "Quite a trip, Princess. So, the great and the near-great could not help you in your quest? Hmmm, small wonder. What made you decide the Lillehammer scene would produce any answers?"

"Oh, honorable Hondo, I did not decide to come here! I had decided to sit on a forgotten beach and not move until I was so moved. That's when a cetacean by trade, a Dolphin, helped me see God again…instead of just seeing ME."

> Off the blast of light from Times Square, a man named Letterman spoke a language I did not understand.

> To which the Shaq slammed the Mouse in a dazzling Disney-moment just to qualify for who knows what?
>
> — Sara

"How moving. Did this, um, Dolphin claim the Godhead?"

Sara giggled, "Oh, quite the contrary. The Dolphin made no claims at all."

"Did this Dolphin have a name? Rather, was this creature very black with only his left eye crowned in white?" Sara gazed wide-eyed and nodded.

Hondo sat back on his spiny tail and guffawed, the leathery plates gaped, clattering with his move. Even the band was distracted by the racket, but they played on.

"Why in God's name did I go away.
Why in heck did I stay.
Still beyond my reach
but in my heart
Are the endless Kerrville skies."

"Oh, quite the contrary. The Dolphin made no claims at all."

Hondo whispered, looking both ways for eavesdroppers. "Star Channel. My old friend. It was *he* who found *you*. Don't you see, my dear. It's all part of the magic. You must be very close to the Spirit Father. Please tell me where that old wave-dancer sent you."

She peered into the smoldering sage. A shadow of sorrow sounded like the gentlest murmur of angel wings beating perfectly in the vault of heaven.

"I stood before the Great Pyramid
An icon, an idol, a fake.
It wasn't holy ground...
But Elvis spoke to me anyway.

Into the Mississippi Delta,
From there I saw the flame,
Sweet sister of the Morning Star
Charity was her name...

Mercury the messenger of night,
Charity the child of light,
Together in the Big Easy,
And no one remembers the day.
Mexican Manuel,
cowboy of the River Walk
Took me to the Nazareth Project,
To show me what is honor.

So the never-ending
Quantum Leap of Faith
Set me in the killing fields
Where the eagle hides her young.

For a moment on the Sunset Strip
Madonna took my hand...
To show me what was gorgeous
In her barren land.

The midnight pilot Strider
Took me on his wings
To a place where lights are liars.
And the soul can never sing.

"

For a moment on the Sunset Strip
Madonna took my hand...
To show me what was gorgeous.
In her barren land.

"

She wept bitterly. And the band played on—

"For going' home I'm helpless,
and stayin' here I'll die
Until my heart
is set free
Under Kerrville sky."

And Hondo nodded knowingly...just as a pizza-faced American burst into the bar yelling, "He won! He won! By gosh, he finally won!"

Big Al...Big Al, the gentle guard of Watts,
He taught me to look beyond
the burning buildings...
To see who was stealing what.

Next stop was a back lot
behind the sacred scene
with the makers of reality
Where the Truth has never been.

— *The Ballad of Sara Doom*

"...and stayin' here I'll die."

Wouldn't you think that a 200-pound armadillo cruisin' through crowded streets of an Olympic Village might make someone gawk? But, *nobody* noticed. By now, Sara was beyond surprise. Way beyond. People have this odd tendency to be less aware of their surroundings the more "self" fills their screen. So be it, she thought. It was snowing again any-

Wouldn't you think that a 200-pound armadillo cruisin' through the crowded streets of an Olympic Village might make someone gawk? But, nobody noticed.

The goal was to raise a million or so for the orphans caught in the insanity of the former Yugoslavic republic. (You know Christian versus Muslim versus...oh, you know the old story).

way, and all she wanted was a simple truth. "How 'bout a 'multi-cultural' *half*-truth," Hondo smirked.

On they went. On they went past a souvenir stand. (Tonya Harding police batons were selling well.). There were, of course, the Thunderbird-swilling drunks and preciously-attired n'er-do-wells mincing along the way. But the most fascinating commotion was the activity surrounding the Sarajevo memorial. Koss, "The Boss," Norway's speed-skating hero, had started the ball rolling when he donated his Olympic Gold Medal cash bonus (well over $30,000) to the effort. The goal was to raise a million or so for orphans created by the insanity infecting this formerly civilized people. (You know Christian versus Muslim versus...oh, you know that tedious story). At any rate, their going was slow. So many celebrities and happenings. Sara was glad she and old Hondo were so invisible.

Still, shouts of "He won! He finally won!" were heard in the streets. Finally, they reached the speed-skating arena. Thousands of people were cheering and chanting.

"Dan! Dan! Dan!"

They arrived just in time to see Dan Jansen waving to the crowd on his victory lap. His wife and family were in tears as he glided by to scoop up his infant child in his arms. Dan and daughter circled the track...a moment of love that little girl would hold on to...forever.

Sara began to cry. Hondo smiled. He knew.

Sara was crying for all her brothers and sisters, from Sarajevo to St. Paul to Sira Lanka to Slippery Rock...all those cold children of this silent generation. She wept because *they* had no fatherly moment of tenderness, of warm masculine love, to hold them tightly against the winter's night until the brightness of morning light would fall upon them as gently as a waltz around an ice rink, held proudly in their father's embrace.

Sara spoke finally, "Take me home, Hondo. I've seen enough. My ethic isn't lost. It's just unwanted and abandoned."

She turned to leave when she felt a large hand on her shoulder. Dan Jansen's eyes smiled. He offered Sara his little daughter and said, "Would you please hold her for me while I go and receive my gold medal?" Off he skated. Cheering rolled over them like crashing waves.

"My daddy's cool."

Sara nodded, "Cool, indeed!"

Jansen beamed as his child returned to his shoulder. Millions felt that little girl's security as she held tight to her Daddy. Millions watched with craving for distant memories, and with a sense of loss. Oh, to feel that way again (or ever)! Sara made her way through the crowd pressing toward the ice rink. She found Hondo swapping jokes with a Norwegian reindeer at the end of the woods.

"Ha, Ha, Ho, Hee…Oh, Ho…Wheew! That was a good one! Bjorn here was just tellin' me the one about Rudolf and Santa and 12 dancin' Chip'n Dale elves…an'…Um… never mind. Ready to go?"

"Go? Where?"

The reindeer spoke to Hondo in Norwegian. He nodded and high-hoved Bjorn. The old 'dillo leaned close to Sara.

"Do you like basketball?"

"What? Is this another Norwegian reindeer-Texas-armadillo-teen-bashing-type joke?!"

"Chill out, Princess! You need a reality check."

"What she needs is a hug." The voice was warm and cheerful and from a gentler quiet time. A tender little elderly lady with rosy cheeks, button nose, kind eyes magnified by wire-framed granny glasses, a quizzical smile, and snow puff hair—all packaged in a state-of-the-art CBS Sports blizzard prototype parka—approached Sara.

She spoke again with her down-on-the-farm-Indiana surety,

"Hi, I'm Dave's Mom."

Yes, it was David Letterman's Mom reporting live from Lillehammer. She hugged Sara in that near-forgotten grandma way. Sara savored the moment.

"See, I told you. A hug a day makes the gloom go away. Bye now."

And off she went to interview Dan Jansen, who was catching a ride on a passing reindeer.

The old 'dillo grinned and nodded.

"I almost forgot that you humans need to connect physical embrace with your emotional bonds."

Sara turned and wiped her eyes.

"The Creator intended it that way."

"Indeed the Creator did, Princess. But we've almost forgotten that touch."

"Each other's? Or the Creator's?"

Sara looked west. The Norwegian moon was a fluorescent blue dish hanging over the Olympic Village. She lifted her hands. *"Yes!"*

> "Take me home, Hondo. I've seen enough. My ethic isn't lost. It's just unwanted and abandoned."

> Millions felt that little girl's pride and joy and secureness as she held tight to her Daddy. Millions watched with envy, and longing, and with a sense of loss. Oh, to feel that way again (or ever).

"I almost forgot that you humans need to connect physical embrace with your emotional bonds."
—Hondo

"Bjorn said the professors were all a'twitter 'bout some author, name of Purebread, Marc Purebread."

Once in a blue moon someone asks the right question, and another gives the right response. And every so often, when hell freezes over like an Olympic speed-skating track, a cold hard surface of man-made reality gets etched with courage and heart from the blades of actual fatherly love. And everyone watches. And everyone wishes...that they could be on their father's heroic shoulders with a multitude of adoring fans crying out his name.

Sara put her hand on Hondo's weary head.

"What was that you said about basketball?"

"Heh, heh, ha...well, it's not the reason we should go to North Carolina, but don't tell the natives that."

"What is the reason?"

"Theology," laughed Hondo.

"Theology?"

"Sure, Christian ethics."

"Is this the joke Bjorn, the reindeer, was telling you?"

"Oh, heavens no. He told me a funny joke. What he *did* tell me was that he overheard some professor-types talking about a conference on Christian ethics happenin' at Duke in North Carolina. Maybe those academic-nuts can help you."

Sara was almost encouraged, "Hondo, do you suppose *they* have my ethic?"

"Hardly. Probably don't even know where *theirs* is...But it doesn't matter. What they *do* have is books...lotza books."

"And that's where my ethic is?"

"No, no, no, Sara...think! These theologians and philosophers and professors of knowledge love books...and authors. Specially live ones. And that's why we're goin' there. They've got a live one. Bjorn said the professors were all a'twitter 'bout some author, name of Purebread, Marc Purebread."

"And this is a good thing?"

"Who knows. All I knows is he's from Texas, has a new book on your generation, and is gonna be talkin' to those eggheads at Duke on Sunday morning."

"Then we should go."

"Well, heck yes, Princess. If things get boring, at least we can see that Blue Devils team play some serious Southern basketball."

Sara and Hondo began laughing uncontrollably when Strider arrived in a sleigh (full of John Wesley and band playing "Carolina on My Mind") pulled by Bjorn. Strider nearly fell on his face in the snow, climbing from the dory.

"Carolina? North Carolina? Durham-Duke-Blue Devils-Carolina?" he asked and then he did a double take.

"Did John Wesley tell you?" Hondo asked.

"No, the reindeer told me, Mr. Talkin' Armadillo. What does **IT** mean, Sara?" Strider asked his young passenger.

"Bjorn's the reindeer, Hondo's not an "it." "Our" means all of us—Duke in North Carolina's where Purebread is. He's a Texan...and do you like basketball?" Sara said in an animated huff.

Strider looked this way, and then that way. He nodded automatically and pretended to smile. It was the face of the clueless.

"Next stop Carolina" was all he could manage.

❝

No, no, no, Sara...think! These theologians and philosophers and professors of knowledge love books...and authors. Specially live ones.   — Hondo

If things get boring, at least we can see that Blue Devils team play some serious Southern basketball.
—Hondo

❞

 **HONDO ZONE**

Culture Zone: Well, first you have to know old Hondo (a good relationship with an iguana or dolphin will do)...or at least believe in the magic of snow and Olympic Peace and Kerrville Sky, Country music and possibilities.

EARTH DAY

She had a lot more irony she wished to try out on an American writer. But, he just walked away, barefoot on the sugar white sand. He didn't know whether to laugh till he cried, or just to go right to the crying part.

HARD. PLAY HARD. TALK HARD. BE HARD. LOOK HARD.

━━━━━━━━━━━━━━━━━━━ "

Longing for the right words, The Writer looked out across Emerald Beach. He knew what he felt. History was surely not flotsam bobbing endlessly on some forgotten seas, waterlogged with the fluid of our failing memories. Surely not. One of those Nova Scotia octogenarian babes broke his concentration.

"Did you hear? Did you hear that your President Nixon died?"

"*My* President Nixon," he thought.

"No ma'am, I didn't hear."

Sensing she had cornered a sucker, she continued, "Oh yes, and on Earth Day to boot. Just imagine the irony."

She waited for his response. She had a lot more irony she hoped to try out on an American writer. But, he just walked away, barefoot on the sugar white sand. He didn't know whether to laugh till he cried, or just to go right to the crying part. "Irony?" he thought. "My Lord, Nixon died...I bet they're saying he will be remembered for opening up China and all that...not Watergate, and Nam, and Kent State, and Checkers... and that everyone will forget. Because history gets kind when no one really thinks that things of the past are relevant. But irony? C'mon."

He walked a few yards out into the emerald ocean. Another dolphin made a breath-taking leap near enough for him to taste the salt spray when its tail slapped.

"So, it's Earth Day, is it? So where's the irony? Thirty years of policies that gouge this planet, and leave you, Mr. Dolphin, in quite a fix. *Earth Day.* The celebration of a wounded orb, hyped by the marketable superficialities of tee shirts, beer cozies, cute little stuffed dolphins, and a few bucks raised for the Rainbow Warrior. Where's the change of heart? Where is the repentance? Where on God's green earth is the shame?"

The sound of chanting voices overcame him. Just down the beach the **National Pro-Am Celebrity Beach Volleyball** extravaganza was underway. Countless sculptured, tanned, near-naked bodies rose and fell to the violent smacking and whacking. **HARD. PLAY HARD. TALK HARD. BE HARD. LOOK HARD.** These were the children of the children who forgot history. And for their children's children's children, they were trapped in this moment.

"It's ironic, you know." **HARD ZONE**

 Culture Zone: That ironic sense that the harder one tries to escape irony, the harder things get.

CHAPTER 2

THE SEVENTIES PRESERVATION SOCIETY
(WHITE DREAMS IN ACADEME)

"Bless our poor benighted souls" was all Strider could say as he (somehow) managed to land "Eagle's Wings" on a deserted highway (somewhere) outside of Durham, North Carolina. It was overcast and the dawn air was thick, like refrigerated mush. The passengers quickly deplaned (or bailed-out) to kiss American soil and thank their lucky stars (if you believe in such magic). Their trip across the Atlantic would have made Lindberg proud, but everyone was too queasy to consider the parallel. Hondo adjusted his Stetson and wondered,

"Being here is good. Yes, but where is *here*?"

As fate would have it (if one believes in such magic), a local tobacco farmer was passing by in his 1963 John Deere.

"Y'all must be lost," he chuckled.

Sara stood up. "Just my ethic, sir. Do you know where a Duke is?"

The farmer removed his cap slowly, scratched his bald spot, replaced the cap and frowned,

"Course I do. Everybody do. Are you all students, Devil fans, or just hippie carpetbaggers?"

John Wesley noticed the Duke University mascot on the old coots' cap, put his arm around his shoulder and whispered Alfred Hitchcock style, "He's a Blue Devils' fan...comes from West Texas. You know the type."

The old man spit a trail of tobacco juice, revealing a toothless grin. Seeming to grasp John Wesley's nonsense, he nodded knowingly. "Well, why didn't ya say so, neighbor? C'mon, I'll haul yer Texas tree-jumper to Durham. (In a hushed tone and not taking his eyes off Hondo, he advised John Wesley), "...ugly, them West Texas boys."

Dodging another spray of Carolina jaw juice, John Wesley patted the old man's shoulder and laughed, "Hondo may look like the north end of a south-bound mule, but he shore does know his hoops!"

" Being here is good. Yes, but where is here? — Hondo "

"YOU'RE GOING TO MISS IT, GREG!"

"Why is the Grand Canyon so unbelievable to modern spectators?"

The Writer considered his own question, but just shook his head in disbelief at what he saw and heard. An impeccably-dressed-for-the-occasion-of-Canyon-touring-twenty-something couple had stepped out of their BMW and rushed to the lookout for a Kodak moment.

There it was.

It was right in front of them.

The light was just right.

Whoops, that eagle might still be in her camera frame. Perfect, perfect.

"Gregie, hurry, honey," she urged.

Greg fiddled with the aperture and setting of the lens.

"You're going to miss it, sweetie," she insisted.

Greg was muttering at the camera.

"You're missing it, darling," she all but shouted.

He fumbled in the camera bag for a tinted lens cover.

"Oh, Greg, you missed it," she yelled at him and stamped off toward the BMW.

He looked up dumbfounded, cursed under his breath and followed her.

The Writer could hear her as they drove off to the next lookout point, "I can't believe you missed it!"

The Writer looked back at the ancient canyon before him. A tear formed as he said,

"You missed it."

 **TIME ZONE**

Culture Zone: Since we've evolved into hurry-up-this-will-only-last-as-long-as-I-am-around Zonies…there is a lingering sense that we missed…something.

CHANNEL SURFING AT THE DUKE MOTEL

While "all the guys" were getting ready in the next room for their big gig that night, Sara sat alone in her sterile suite. All the furnishings had that Barbie Motel cardboard box touch and all the appeal of a pastel post-modern nightmare. She sat cross-legged on the floor between a tacky bed and a television that was bolted to a Formica-covered chest of sorts. So out of her element that she could have screamed, she pointed the remote at the TV.

"What would make people create such an atmosphere?" she thought.

CLICK...
CNN "This is Headline News, a CNN Network."

"Today outside Newark, New Jersey, yet another Amtrak train accident. The Silver Streak derailed...bodies strewn...damage in the millions of dollars... Spokesman for the company called the incident just more 'bad luck.'"

CLICK...
"O Spirit Father, is no one responsible? For *anything*?" she said, closing her eyes tightly.

CLICK...
"And now back to the Young and the Restless..."
"Baby, you know I love you..."

CLICK...
"Could this be our way now? Hollowness without shame?" Sara cried.

CLICK...
"This is Larry King Live...you're on the air, Truckee, California...and we're speaking with Fawlin Star...'Ms Starr, you make me so mad. Why don't you stand up for yourself?"

"I, I have been a *victim* my whole life...my mother made me feel...and then she made me..."

CLICK...

"Do we really not believe there is space between us? Are we such clones of each other that we can actually blame someone else's words or thoughts for causing our hand to slap another's face?" Sara wondered.

CLICK...

...spokesman for the company called the incident just more "bad luck."

86

> We pledge ourselves to liberate all our people from the continuing bondage of poverty, deprivation, suffering, gender and other discrimination. — Mandela

> There in a land where tens of thousands had given their lives for that moment, the sun is shining.

NO APARTHEID ZONE

Culture Zone: That most miraculous of places where forgiveness outweighs hatred, and humility makes the sun shine.

"Dan Rather, CBS News. Today in Pretoria, South Africa, history has been made…Nelson Mandela, leader of the ANC, former political prisoner of nearly three decades for his stand against Apartheid in South Africa is now its first black president! Mandela spoke after taking the oath of office…'We have, at last, achieved our political emancipation. We pledge ourselves to liberate all our people from the continuing bondage of poverty, deprivation, suffering, gender and other discrimination.'"

"Mandela's Second Deputy President, former South African President, Frederik deKlerk, stood by his side. F. W. deKlerk, the man who drove the process to free elections, of whom the man who succeeded deKlerk said…'(he) is one of the greatest sons of our soil.'"

"Mandela went on to say, 'Let us forget the past. What is done is done. Now that we have won, we have forgotten our differences and will move to heal the wounds of the past…'"

Dan Rather rambled on, but Sara did not hear. She stood, mouth agape, and stared. Soon tears streamed down her cheeks and fell on the mauve indoor-outdoor carpet. She raised her palms to the sparkle stryo-sprayed ceiling and prayed. It was Day. The sun was shining in some place called Pretoria. It was Day.

"O dearest Spirit Father, thank you, thank you for one more Day. There in a land where tens of thousands had given their lives for that moment, the sun is shining. There where a lone man from the ruling class caused something miraculous to happen for a people—and a man—of different color, knowing it would mean the loss of personal power, the sun is blazing. There, where a gentle black-skinned elder of his land, who was jailed inhumanely, spoke of forgiveness: Daylight had fought its way through the night. And he challenged the world, 'Out of the experience of an extraordinary human disaster that lasted far too long must be born a society of which all humanity will be proud.'"

Sara wept. CBS cameras were panning the gathered great and near great. There was Cuba's Castro next to Palestine's Arafat…and standing next to Tipper Gore was (you got it) the Reverend Jesse Jackson—(they were conversing). Sara laughed out loud.

"Still discussing the value of things, no doubt," she thought. There was someone who resembled David Letterman's Mom interviewing Madonna, but Sara wasn't sure. She wasn't sure, but for the first time since she left the Badlands, Sara Doom felt part of the planet again. It felt good.

"Sara!"

"C'mon, hon, we'll be late!"

It was John Wesley and the boys at the door. Sara stole one more look at the miracle from South Africa. Mandela spoke, "Today, all of us, by our presence here, confer glory and hope to newborn liberty."

ANOTHER PHOTO OP FOR AUNT JEN

Sunset at the Grand Canyon makes most visitors pause and contemplate things they might otherwise not take time to consider. Why? After all, it is just the sun moving beyond the horizon. Nothing so special about that, is there? Other than the fact that colors outside the spectrum appear, vistas change in a blink of an eye, and the largest most vivid and awesome 360-degree panorama of not-man-made beauty completely surrounds the view like a rainbow tornado—well, other than that, it is just another sunset.

The Writer and company sat near the edge of the main lookout and simply stared westward. Nearly a hundred tourists had gathered. No one spoke in whispers. People hurried to the railing and behaved as though they had come to watch an atomic blast.

A colorfully-dressed woman began herding her young toward the edge. She set up her camera on its tripod and hollered to her children to get in the picture before the sun went down. After each child posed with the setting sun and her flash blipped uselessly, she would exclaim, "Oh, Aunt Jen will just love that one!"

She seemed discontent with something she saw in her lens and spoke loudly to The Writer's sister,

"Excuse me, Miss. Miss, could you please move your leg…it's in the way."

His sister looked behind her some fifty miles into the distance and moved her leg.

The woman's last flash went off, and she began to shoo her family toward the parking lot.

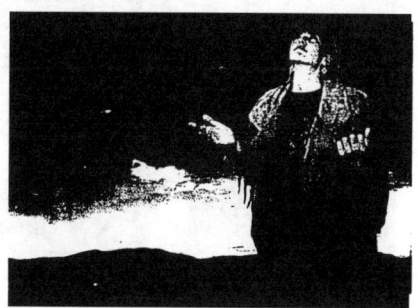

"Excuse me Miss. Miss, could you please move your leg…it's in the way."

His sister looked behind her some fifty miles into the distance and moved her leg.

"Okay, we got that. If we hurry, we'll get back to town and miss the dinner rush."

His sister said, "Wonder if she knows the flash completely blotted out the background in her pictures?"

"I wonder if she knows she left her purse," laughed her husband.

"I think Aunt Jen is glad she's not here," said The Writer's wife.

"Excuse me, Sis, but do you think you could move your leg a little...it's blocking my view," The Writer said.

The sun went down. The show was over. Everyone just turned from the rail and went away.

And after they had all gone...a solitary silhouette walked to the Canyon rim...pointing her finger she spoke..."The language of angels. Thank you."

The sun went down. The show was over. Everyone just turned from the rail and went away.

"

 SHOW'S OVER ZONE

Culture Zone: Time after time, we find ourselves at the big show, the long-waited-for-moment, and we want to take our picture and move along to the next entertainment destination...but after we're gone, the show goes on.

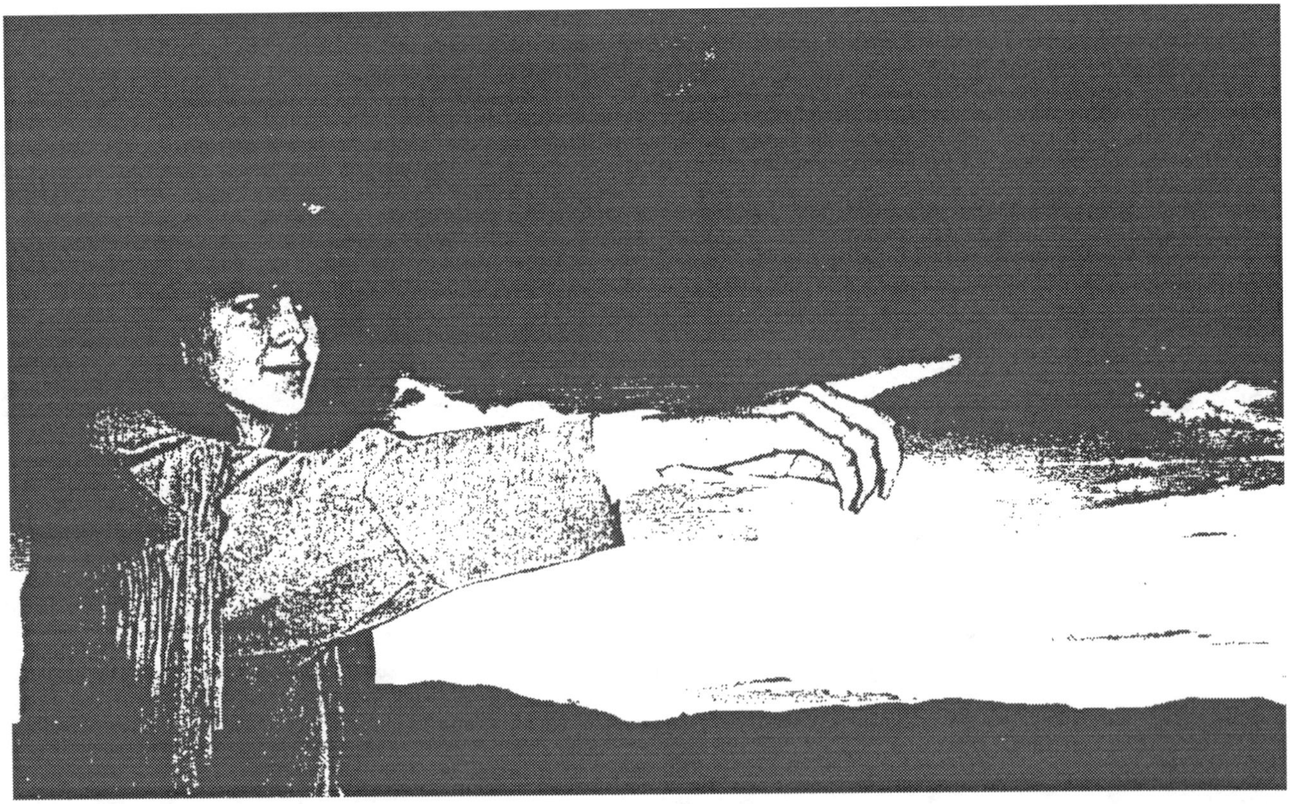

THAT EVENING AT DUKE CHAPEL

The 200-voice Duke Divinity School choir had just sung Wesley's "How Firm a Foundation" when Sara and Hondo found a spot near the back by a quiet young boy with a sparkling toddler on his lap. The little girl kept saying, "When do we get French fries?"

The keynote speaker stood in a magnificent pulpit. Even with his mistaken combination of clergy robes and doctoral hood, the man was out of place in *this* place. Shoulder-length hair flopped this way and that as he spoke, and his right hand nervously stroked his mustache or adjusted wire-rimmed glasses. But his voice was warm and it stuck to the cold chapel walls.

> *"Whose voice is missing among us?*
> *Where do we go to find it …*
> *and learn from it…*
> *and claim it for the church."*
>
> — Purebread

The little girl squirmed on her brother's lap.

"Is he in a bad move?"

"No, Sparky. He's not in a bad mood. Try and be quiet. Mommy will be back in a minute. Try and listen…quietly."

"I wanna see Markie!"

Sara could not take her eyes off the enchanting child. Sparky noticed Sara was chewing gum and asked, "Candy?"

The boy looked embarrassed and explained, "I'm sorry. She wants some of your gum."

Sara was pleased and dug into her backpack. "Here, angel."

The little girl took the stick of gum and said matter of factly, "Not Angel. Sparky, thank you."

The speaker continued.

"Whose voice is missing among us?

Where do we go to find it …
and learn from it…
and claim it for the church."
— Purebread

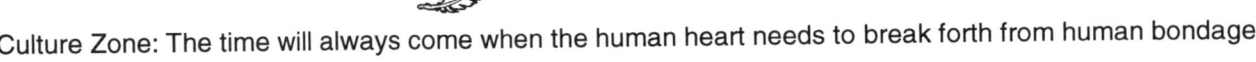

HEART ZONE

Culture Zone: The time will always come when the human heart needs to break forth from human bondage.

"ONE, FROM THE HEART"

(Marc Purebread's presentation to the Duke Theological Conference on Christian Ethics)

"Nowhere in our society are expectations higher and anxiety levels greater than among our teenagers. Madison Avenue develops the nation's ad campaigns around their changing desires. Wall Street counts on their expendable income. Hollywood cash registers hum on their youthful tastes. And the church tries to play catch-up. All the while we press on toward an uncertain new century, and the litany of confusion sounds something like this:

> Hollywood cash registers hum on their youthful tastes.

"One morning a woman in Chicago wakes up early to muffled noises outside her bedroom window. She peers out and sees six teenagers quickly stripping her car of all that is valuable from hub caps to CD player. Weary, she asks the police, 'What did I ever do to those kids to have them treat me this way?'

"We visited with two college kids recently who are near graduation. I asked them to fill me in on the state of the church on campus. The history major said it was like a 'welfare state.' 'Too many folks on the rolls are getting something for nothing.' The economics major summed it up: 'It's like most modern institutions with a high public profile and low consumer returns.' Neither of these young people have jobs lined up after graduation.

"Trends seem to merit predictions that by the year 2000 there may be as many college graduates living back home with their parents as those who find jobs. Yet a recent *Harper's Magazine Integral* states that since 1988 the number of American college students who have their own credit cards has soared 37%. It could be 50% in the next five years.

> Experts who look into such matters conclude that by the year 2000 there may be as many college graduates living back home with their parents as those who find jobs.

"Racial violence is on the rise in public school systems. A downtown school in Houston, Texas, employs over twenty armed guards. Yet that same school won last year's football title with a racially-balanced team. Litanies of fear, mixed messages and failed solutions haunt us. We are in a desperate search for the simplicity of sensible behavior, played out before us with absolute answers that defy complex realities. And we want winners. And we want security at any cost. And, we want it now! Yet in the haste, the price may be our heart.

"When searching for heroes and winners these days, our criteria seems to rely on the questionable memories of the goodness of days gone by, mixed with an emotional response no deeper than passing fads. We are rooted in the soil of what feels good, as though it will get us through the

92

dark night of our nation's soul. By contrast, God's criteria looks into the heart."

Sparky was agitated. "He's in a bad move."

"Sshhh...he's almost done and Mommy will be here soon, I hope."

"Why does your sister feel the speaker is in a bad mood?"

"Cause he hates this kinda stuff."

"How do you know?"

The little girl climbed unexpectedly on Sara's lap. "It's Markie."

Sara looked confused. Sparky began digging in Sara's backpack. The boy spoke. "The speaker is our dad."

"Markie," said Sparky.

Sara smiled as the little girl finally noticed Hondo, who was napping.

"Manatee!" she shouted with joy.

Hondo batted his sleepy eyelids.

"Who's the rugrat, Sara?"

Marc Purebread was finishing, "What of Christian moral ethics? Are its constants or absolutes possible today? What does a Christian ethic look like? For God's sake, traditional ethics are so out of touch with the crises in our streets and government and churches and our homes that we might be better off consulting a Navajo medicine man than Ethics professors."

Sparky looked into Sara's dark eyes, "See, Markie's in a bad move," she giggled. "Mommy, mommy, look...a manatee," she gestured wildly in Hondo's general direction. Sparky's mother was an elegant and delicate woman of the sort seen in beatnik paintings popular on Paris' Left Bank. She held a cheerful infant dressed in an 1890s manner and was accompanied by a miniature preteen girl with huge clear blue eyes. They all stared at Hondo. All he could do was tip his hat and drawl, "Evenin' ma'am. Please don't be alarmed. Me an the boys are just tryin' to get this Indian Princess home via Texas. Thought maybe the Rev. Doctor Purebread might help some hometown boys outta this God-forsaken place."

The woman glanced from Hondo to her child on Sara's lap, to the young boy, then to the pulpit where the speaker had just said, "Thank ya'll again for your gracious reception of my book and my vocalized exasperation (laughter and clapping enlivened the chapel)...I'll be headin' back to Texas tonight with my family before this conference ends, so I leave you with this prayer...God grant us the supernatural gift of humility...the

> And we want winners. And we want security at any cost. And, we want it now! Yet in the haste, the price may be our heart.

What of Christian ethics? Are its constants or absolutes possible today? What does a Christian ethic look like? For God's sake…

wisdom to learn from our own history…the ability to change…and the courage to stand with those who cannot. Thank you."

When the ovation began, the woman spoke directly to Hondo, "Please don't apologize, Mr. Manatee (she winked at Sparky). We would love to have you accompany us home. They'd eat you alive here. And I know my husband will be pleased to meet you. Once he gets over his bad move."

"I wanna see Markie, Mommy."

"We've met, yer husband and I…sort of," drawled Hondo.

Sara stood holding the child. She bowed to the woman. "I am so grateful. The eagle told me I would find my ethic."

"My name is Skipper. I don't know about finding your ethic, but we can certainly help you get home, child. What is your name?"

"Sara Doom."

Skipper embraced Sara. Sparky wiggled down and began trying to sit on Hondo. The baby cooed. The young boy began gathering purses and backpacks. The preteen, pretty-as-a-picture girl took Sara's hand. "My name's Doll. Do you like to play?"

Sara smiled.

Skipper made sure everyone was accounted for and said, looking at Sara, "Come on, children, it's time to go home."

The audience was still clapping as the Duke Divinity School choir began Luther's "A Mighty Fortress is Our God." Hondo shook his head, "Dang old songs; John Wesley shoulda played here."

" ────────────

God grant us the supernatural gift of humility…the wisdom to learn from our own history…the ability to change…and the courage to stand with those who cannot. Thank you."
—Purebread

────────────── "

"Dang old songs; John Wesley shoulda played here."

THEOLOGY ZONE

Culture Zone: It is that one 'OLOGY' that really bakes our biscuits…no one gets it. Except every-so-often we get a piece of God's mind, even in Chapel.

```
…Update…Doom update…Update…There has
been an Elvis sighting…Film at
Eleven…Update…Doom update…There has
```

94

A MESSAGE FROM MOTHER MARY

Out past the Petrified Forest and Painted Desert, the thunder rolls and roars with sounds no one is there to hear. Clouds form in an instant—and vanish as quickly. Dust devils skip across the highway and swirled across the low-lying scenery. Along the way travelers may rest at curio shops or even solitary wayside stops. Each one holds claim to a small secret of the universe. There are actual-factual bits of petrified wood to be had, or you can get photographed with an old Indian sitting in the shade of a rusted gas station canopy.

The Writer and company were standing on the porch of one such place, sipping cokes while watching the lightning storm a hundred miles to the east.

"Look, I bought this old picture frame from the attendant," his wife said.

They were admiring her $5 find when a van pulled into the station. Painted meticulously in three-foot letters on its side was the message:

"The Virgin Mary has a Message for You...Dial 1-800 (something).

No one laughed. They just looked at each other.

The Writer dug into his pocket for a quarter and flipped it into the air wondering if anyone would catch it.

MARY-AND-ALL-ANGELS ZONE

Culture Zone: Even in the desert you have that old feeling that someone has a message for you.

REVENGE OF THE VILLAGE PEOPLE

By the time Sara and the Purebread entourage had escaped the crowds and made their way to the lobby, Marc arrived panting and dripping with ecclesiastical sweat. He hugged Skipper vigorously and his gathering of children, his manner not unlike that of Patton inspecting the troops. Then, he turned to the strangers.

"Whoa! And these are...?"

In her motherly fashion, Skipper patted his robed and hooded shoulder, "These are ours. They'll be our guests for a few days. This is ..."

Sara, impatient, interrupted.

"Oh, Reverend Doctor Purebread, this is...I mean, I am Sara, Sara Doom. You see, I've lost my ethic and I've just looked *everywhere* for it and thenIkeptmeetingtheoddestofpeopleinthestrangestofplacesanditisalways coldandmostlysnowingandthesunjustwon'tshineexceptintthatSouth AfricaplacebutthenImetHondo. Oh dear, this is Hondo...."

The Reverend Doctor Purebread, his wife and children and (especially) Hondo were staring at Sara in befuddlement. She blushed with embarrassment. Sensing her need for relief, Skipper's elbow cracked Marc in the ribs. After his confused glance, he stammered "Um, yes dear...I see...you are Sara Doom and this...I mean...he-she-it...um...your friend here is Hondo....," he said, squinting at the armadillo with confused recognition.

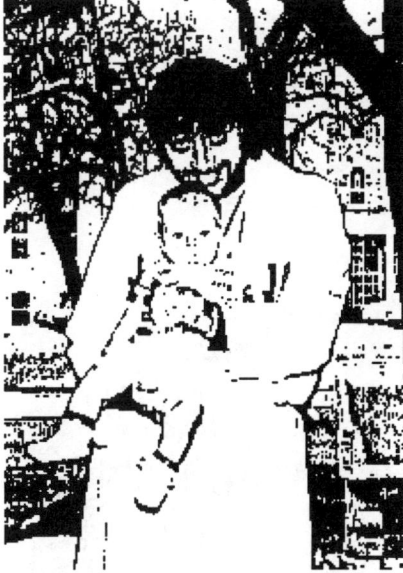

Oh, Reverend Doctor Purebread, this is...I mean, I am Sara, Sara Doom. You see, I've lost my ethic and I've just looked everywhere for it...
— Sara

"He's a manatee, Markie," Sparky laughed.

"Ahhh, right. Glad to have both of you coming home with us."

Marc adjusted his glasses, smiled in his absent-minded-professor way, gave his wife a "help me" look and waited for further instructions. Barely able to keep from laughing at her husband's awkward posturing, Skipper broke the silence.

"Honey, this child needs to speak with you, and Mr. Hondo and his company need a ride back to Texas. Okay?"

Purebread cleared his throat.

"Makes sense to me."

Hondo couldn't believe his ears. "It does?"

"What's so cool about those fools? Seventies were notin' but a buncha polyester-rayon-dacron-wide-la-peled-disco-deadhead-wangers with all the class God gave an armadillo!"
— Starbuck

"I told you he would understand," Skipper assured him.

"Beats anything I've ever seen," answered Hondo.

(Beats anything *he's* seen?! thought Marc.)

"Wow! Cool! The 70s Preservation Society!"

The out-of-place surprise of his statement was as mood-clearing as the cracking pre-pubescence of the voice that muttered it. Sparky's older brother, who had been so solicitous of Sara in the chapel, held up a magazine and laughed. He explained, with enthusiasm,

"Sez right here in my *Rolling Stone*, 'The 70s Preservation Society' presents the songs that made a misunderstood decade memorable. Look at the clothes they're wearin'. Cool, huh?"

A menacing voice came from behind the boy. "What's so cool about those fools? Seventies were nuttin' but a buncha polyester-rayon-dacron-wide-lapeled-disco-deadhead-wangers with all the class God gave an armadillo!"

Skipper interceded. "Watch your language in front of your little sisters, and try to be civil. We have guests." Her raised eyebrows noted Sara and Hondo.

The dark-haired 20-something man tried to be cool. Couldn't.

"Ooops."

"This is our oldest son, Starbuck," Marc explained.

"They're *not* cool?" asked his little brother.

"He's in a bad move," Sparky added.

"Didya bring us a present from your concert?" Doll asked, jumping into his arms.

Starbuck laughed and set the little girl down. He stood almost a head taller than anyone else. His long hair and three-day beard framed a killer smile and liquid blue eyes.

"Sorry, Mom…it's just…*that* is one major crustation. You gotta be Hondo, man," as he gave him a high five. "The band that stole your name fronted for me tonight. Good to be with some Texas boys on the road."

Sara watched his every move. This Adonis figure reminded her of the great Stone Warrior, who presideded over the last of the spirit eagles. His manner mirrored the prevailing culture, but he submerged within his demeanor (as did the rest of his family), the life of an old soul, one not yet disconnected from the civilized world's history without crushing the quest for personal freedom. Starbuck gave Doll and Sparky and his little brother trinkets, talismans of the night's victory. Saltwater taffy, it was. His mother cradled the baby. The family laughed and hugged and truly enjoyed their peaceful moment. Marc was on his cellular phone, nodding and arguing with hands lashing the air in frustration. Noting Sara's haunting stare, Starbuck addressed his mother.

"Who's the waif?"

"Her name's Sara," Hondo interjected.

"She's my friend," added Sparky, mouth overflowing with candy.

"Sorry. Just looks like..."

"A lost child, Mr. Starbuck. Your little sister looks like a Precious Moments doll, and you look like a Cro-Magnon Hell's Angel...," Hondo said.

"And you look like a stuffed artichoke with a thyroid problem. So what's your point, 'dillo?" Starbuck shot back in his face.

"Manatee," Sparky corrected him.

"My point is, what we look like has precious little to do with who we are inside," Hondo smiled pleasantly (for a 'dillo, that is).

Starbuck laughed. "I love it. An Aristotelian armadillo. Sorry, honey, I'm just a little full of...full of myself," he said to Sara.

"Same thing," muttered his little brother.

"Starbuck, Sir. Do you know where my—our—ethic is?" asked Sara.

He frowned and studied her briefly.

"Look, I'm just a post-modern-deconstructuralist Rocker from the Texas Hill Country, but I have my suspicions that your ethic isn't anywhere around these parts..."

"Then you'll help me find it?" Sara said, hopefully.

"We all will, dear," Skipper said, hugging her shoulder.

Starbuck's little brother pointed to his magazine and shouted, "Cool! What's disco fever, Starbuck?"

"De-evolution, little brother. C'mon, let's split."

> "My point is, what we look like has precious little to do with who we are inside," Hondo smiled pleasantly.
>
> Starbuck laughed, "I love it. An Aristotelian armadillo. Sorry honey, I'm just a little full of...full of myself."
> — Starbuck

DISCO ZONE

Culture Zone: Oh, it's just another one of those moments when you feel like marketed surroundings around you are trying to drown out reality with brash lighting, loud techno-music and mediocrity.

The convertible Rabbit crested a rise on I-10, and El Paso stretched out below as far as you could see. At night there are ten thousand thousand points of light spread in all directions forever. The Interstate hugs the mountainside for 30 miles while the light show blinks rhythmically below.

The Writer turned to his wife and said, "There are over 40,000 college students down there somewhere, wishing they were anywhere but there. And see all those blue-looking lights? That's the other side of the Rio Grande River, Juarez, Mexico. Over there are a million Mexicans wanting to be over here."

The car carried them away from the city, and she looked back at the dull glow behind them.

"I wonder if they know what's stopping them," she asked.

"A muddy ditch full of water," was all he said.

"

And see all those blue-looking lights? That's the other side of the Rio Grande River, Juarez, Mexico. Over there are a million Mexicans wanting to be over here."

 **NO CROSSING ZONE**

Culture Zone: We choose not to cross borders we've made because we fear what lies between there and here.

CHAPTER 3
"NUCLEAR DISASTER"
(Luckenbach, K-SKY, Redneck Rock, and a Party of **Favorites**)

The Writer picked up his study's phone. It was Father O'Magolly, his old friend from St. Hillarians. "Howdy, Father...oh just one of those days when I've had people crawlin' in and out of my head like earwigs," he said and ranted some more.

The old priest finally laughed and said, "It sounds as if you've had more opportunities than time today."

The Purebread family, Sara Doom, the Hondo band, and a party of favorites stood on the edge of a small airfield like sentinels in the mist "Waiting for Godot." It could have been a depressing occasion had the Purebread kids not turned it into a Kodak moment with their snappy repartee.

"What this place needs is some Christmas lights, at least a few lava lamps...I mean could it be more dreary?" Starbuck said while lighting a small cigar.

"Yucky! Yucky, Starbuck," Sparky shouted and fanned the foul smoke away from her face.

"Hey, unfair, Skipper! How come Starbuck gets to smoke in front of our babies and I can't listen to my music," Wild Bill wanted to know. Skipper shot Starbuck that Look just as he was thumping his younger brother on the back of his head. He crushed out the smoldering black cigar and smiled.

"Sorry, Mom, I was overcome by insensitivity."

"And I'm overcome with nausea," declared an elegant young woman who stepped from behind Starbuck after pinching the beejeburs out of his side.

"Ouch! Darn it, Autumn, I've worked hard on my love handles, girl!" Starbuck whined as he felt a rising welt.

Skipper hugged her daughter. They stood arm-in-arm, laughing at Starbuck as he nursed this latest result of sibling taunting. In the half-light of moon and halogen beams, the two women resembled the Judds taking a curtain call. It was hard to say who was mother, who was daughter. Yet the surrounding crowd of children made it obvious that this was what love looked like.

Sorry, Mom, I was overcome by insensitivity.

— Starbuck
"

"'IT…has no dog-nab desire to be kept…even by a Precious Moments doll and her merrier-than-a-sit-com family…Miss! And before ya'll go callin' something gross, ya outta go a little lighter on the mascara and blush, baby!" —Hondo

Autumn brushed back her auburn hair and picked up her little sister, Sparky. "Sissy, Sissy…we do have a manatee…and my friend, Saryboom," the little girl exclaimed with wiggles and grins. Autumn tried to find answers in her mother's face. "Saryboom?"

Before Skipper could adequately explain their air travel situation and guest list, Sara and Hondo emerged from the mist. Skipper's oldest child gave Sara a casual nod and then looked (with what the Purebread kids called "classic Autumn disdain") toward the old armadillo. She noted Hondo's smirk, and matched him glare for glare. Finally, she appealed to her mother with feigned indignation. "Oh *gross*, Mother! Pleaaase tell me *this* is not going home with us? You're not going to let Sparky keep it, are you?"

Skipper tried to hide her amusement when Hondo shot back, "'IT…has no dog-nab desire to be kept…even by a Precious Moments doll and her merrier-than-a-sit-com family…*Miss*! And before ya'll go callin' anybody gross, ya gotta go a little lighter on the mascara and blush, baby!"

Autumn and Hondo grunted sounds that meant, "Yeech!" as they turned and stomped away, not unlike frustrated duelers whose pistols misfired.

Sara and Skipper could not stifle their laughter. They kept on chuckling as everyone boarded the "Eagles Wings" and kept having giggle fits until the other passengers had fallen asleep somewhere over Alabama. Sara had been cradling the baby. She handed her to Skipper and sat beside her. After a memorable smile, she spoke with her eyes closed.

"Your family…your husband and your children…they remind me of the stories Wally Skydancer has told me about my people. They, they are gone now…."

Skipper arranged the sleeping infant on the seat next to her and smiled, "Oh, we're a tribe, all right."

"Yet, a good one. Are there others, out there…like yours?" Sara asked, her eyes still shut.

Skipper got completely attentive, matching the young woman's serious tone. "Do you have no family, child?"

Tears formed in the creases of Sara's closed eyes. "Oh, Mrs. Skipper Purebread, I am so blessed to have a large family circle…I have Wally Skydancer and Mr. Mercury, Charity, Mr. Big Al, and Strider, Hondo, John Wesley and the Stone Warrior…We would exchange life itself for each other. But, the circle is incomplete…(she sniffed away a tear). In search of my lost ethic…the quest for that excellent thing…everyone's circle is incomplete. Except with the Purebread tribe…and, of course, Mr. Hondo."

Skipper took a sip of hot tea to reflect. "If God has brought you to us, dear, as is usually the case, then God will surely give you the necessary understanding. But please remember, if anything unusual is going on with this tribe of ours, it is founded on some simple truths...

> *"We love each other enough to be honest...*
> *We respect each other enough to listen...*
> *We like each other enough to be patient...*
> *And we keep a good sense of the absurd.*

"Being human is hard enough without complicating matters by setting expectations that do not allow for mistakes. And being a family, especially one of our size, is impossible if each member does not know where they stand, what is reasonable, and has a structure they can always rely upon. There's nothing magical about being a Purebread."

Sara slowly opened her wet eyes and looked at the sleeping child. "There lies the magic."

The airplane banked toward Texas, and Sara said (to Sara),

> *"If I'm supposed to enjoy every minute...*
> *every breath of life...*
> *even the daybreak's shaky moment...*
> *Someone needs to take the time ♪ ♫*
> *to show me how.*
> *How do I enjoy what I do not understand?*
> *...if no one understands that I do not...*
> *understand?*
> *Please?"*

> — *The Ballad of Sara Doom*

And from somewhere in Eagles Wings' back end, someone was dozing off to a Letterman rerun.

"Top ten signs that there are too many people on this planet...This list just faxed in from the home office in Sioux City, Iowa:
Number 6...
There are so many extra people that
Donahue can start killing them on TV...
And the number one sign there are too many people on the planet—
There is now a two-year wait to date Madonna."

Sara wept.

And Skipper held her.

"Eagles Wings" banked west above a gentle rise of smoky blue-green mountains. Strider could not find the airstrip. Starbuck, acting as copilot, pointed at the morning star. "There, good buddy. See it?"

> **"**
> We love each other enough to
> be honest...
> We respect each other enough
> to listen...
> We like each other enough to
> be patient...
> And we keep a good sense of
> the absurd. —Skipper
> **"**

T★E★X★A★S

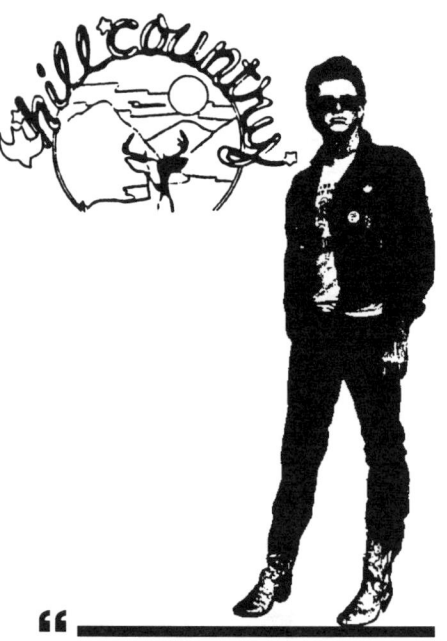

"
Well, it ain't Shangri-La, but it's Texas…closest thing to heaven
"

Strider took off his mirrored shades and looked hard at the star. He turned to his copilot. "And your point is?"

"Why, it's right under it, big fella," laughed Starbuck. And there, appearing like Brigadoon in the Scottish mist was a glimmering diamond below. Strider shook his head and replaced his glasses. The plane geared downward and landed effortlessly. It was not yet dawn, but it would be soon.

"De-planing" looked like an evacuation from Noah's Ark. Children (of all shapes and sizes), band members (with various hair styles), musical instruments that resembled giraffes and hippos, the inevitable baggage required for airborne infants, Strider shading his eyes from the runway lights, the Reverend and Mrs. Purebread (sleeping babies in arms) and finally Hondo and Sara Doom. They were greeted by dogs yapping, birds squalling, more dogs yelping, and two ranch hands, Poncho and Gabriel, laughing and hugging Purebreads. As stuff and people were loaded into two safari-type vehicles, Sara spoke to Hondo. "What could this marvelous place be?"

"Well, it may not be Shangri-La, but it's Texas…closest thing to heaven," Hondo said yawning.

Sara smiled. "Then the sun will soon shine on us."

The vehicles drove an impossible path through a rugged countryside. There was much cheer aboard each of them. (The sounds of HOME.) The Purebread compound could be seen in a valley below, illuminated by ten million-million stars. Their house was the largest log cabin Sara could imagine, and surrounding buildings created the image of a Tolkien village hidden in the forest of time and fond memory. A sign greeted them, *"Welcome to Ransom, Texas, home of the Purebread Ranch, St. Francis Starlite Cathedral, Luchenbach Memorial Trading Post and Coffee House, and K-SKY Radio (voice of the free world)."* The last five words were obviously painted after the sign had been erected.

The Rovers had barely stopped before their passengers moved into the arms of a small greeting party. Sara sensed they were the indigenous peoples of this land. Sara stood in awe near the center of this small community. Not knowing where to look, her eyes met Skipper's who smiled as if to say, "It's okay, sweetheart. Your journey is near its end."

As she climbed the red pine porch stairs, Sara saw Hondo moving toward the woods. She called to him, "Noble friend! Must you leave?"

Hondo turned slowly, showing his weariness. "You go on in there, child. It's time for human stuff like baths and dinner with napkins. I can only take so much of *Homo sapiens*, no offense intended. Besides, I gotta go see an old coyote air jockey I know about his deplorable taste in music. Don't worry, I'll catch up with you before you leave." The old 'dillo raised his head to the sky and snorted, "Nothing like getting civilization outta your system. Ahh." He wandered off into the darkness snickering.

Later, Sara awoke with a start. Was it all a dream, she wondered. The smell of bacon and strong coffee filled her senses. Looking around, she saw an Alice-in-Wonderland room overflowing with delightful stuffed animals and curious dolls from many lands. The overstuffed feather bed creaked in a friendly way as she swung her legs over its edge. Something was different. It was familiar, but...different. The past few days whirled in her head like a dust devil. Then she knew—Sara snapped her head toward the window. In one motion, she threw back the curtain and opened the shutters. The moment pushed the solar system's Pause button ever so briefly that few would have noticed. "It's here!" Sara cried.

Before her, the sun was mounting a burst of life behind the Texas hills. From the farthest reaches in the East a phantasm of umber, burnt umber, molten gold and quicksilver pulsed on mountain crests, their silhouette a watershed between earth and space. Above them rose the endless sky ready to surrender her starry night to the Fiery King.

"Dawn! Dearest God, dawn!" Sara fled the room, dancing. She dashed into the kitchen and nearly knocked Skipper down with a bear hug. "It's dawn! It's really dawn!"

Skipper held her at arms length and laughed. "I'll hold your breakfast on the stove."

Above them rose the endless sky ready to surrender her starry night to the Fiery King.

Sparky tugged on Sara's sleeve. "Take me with you, Saryboom...I'm already done with my eating."

Sara noticed two older women in the kitchen giggling and speaking in a tongue familiar to her. There was also a tall young woman with long jet black hair flowing over rough buckskins leaning against the stove sipping coffee. She held out her hand and shook Sara's firmly.

"Jyssy Joshua. Heard all about your adventure. I'd like to talk to you later about a tune that might suit your story."

Skipper patted Sara on the shoulder. "Jyssy is a singer, Sara, and these are our friends, Maria Angelica and Firewalking Woman." The women bowed and smiled and bowed some more. Jyssy Joshua ran her fingers through her mane of silken hair and took another sip of coffee.

SANCTUARY ZONE

Culture Zone: Close your eyes and imagine that perfect place of safety, warmth, and well being…yes, it is the place where your voice is born…it is the zone of worship.

"I've been searchin' my whole life to make some sense for our people… our generation. We know the music…We can sense it in the air's despair. But baby, I tell ya…We don't have the words—the story that's ours… Words that seek us out, and take us to each other…with love…till now… I've come to sing your song for them…*The Ballad of Sara Doom."*

Sara was frozen. She watched Jyssy's lips but heard her own melody coming from this beautiful dark woman. She heard music. Skipper interrupted. "We can all talk later. You'd better hurry if you're going to catch the show."

Sparky began to protest, "I wanna see Markie! I wanna see him and the animals make sun."

Sara scooped up the little girl and left the women behind.

"Is just over there…" Sparky said.

"On my hill."

Sara climbed effortlessly in the invigorating freshness of predawn. With Sparky's navigation they reached "her spot." It was a dish-shaped rock in a cushion of wildflowers. Standing a few dozen yards below them on a grassy slope, the Reverend Dr. Purebread was reading from a well-worn Bible. He was wearing a simple black cassock unbuttoned from throat to ankle. Underneath he wore a starched white oxford cloth shirt (his Sunday-go-to-meetin' one), rancher's Wrangler jeans and lizard boots. Over the cassock was a floor-length multicolored Peruvian stole; from his neck hung a stylized Jerusalem cross.

There was the sound of a choir. But there was no choir. There were some sheep, a few squirrels, his horse, assorted and sleeping ranch hounds, an exquisite sable border collie sitting at attention before Marc, a small herd of llama, countless birds and rabbits and mice, a large parrot, and an old armadillo who was coming their way.

"Lookit! Lookit! Your manatee!" Sparky shouted with glee.

Hondo snorted to cover a chuckle. "Well, been called worse, I guess." He arranged his old bones beside Sara, out of the child's reach, and grumbled. "Gettin' too old for all this movin' around crap. Umph. Looks like you made it, Princess. Ole' Doc Purebread's gonna bring up the sun, kinda Orpheus-like."

The dawn seemed spellbound between time and space. Sara felt slightly uneasy. There was a slight quiver in her voice when she spoke. "W-where are we? I, I m-mean w-whaat is this place?"

"It's the St. Francis Starlite Cathedral, if you please," said Sparky matter-of-factly as she scrunched closer to Sara.

"Oh?" Sara said, a bit confused.

"The little munchkin's correct. Welcome to the Greatest Show on Earth, I think it goes. Marc Purebread likes to come out here, when he can, and preach to the animals-earth-wind-and-skies—Bubba-land's own Dr. Doolittle. My domino partner over there settin' up that darn fool radio equipment broadcasts the whole mess by K-SKY underground radio via some far-blessed-away sub-com satellite up there near the Big Dipper. It's all very technical, of course. Probably illegal, but his motives are pure 'nuf. Anyway, this child's daddy comes out here from time to time just to make sure the sun will break the grasp of darkness. Or, so he says. He can count on a captive audience. Even a few of you humans show up. But it's a darn good show."

It's all very technical, of course. Probably illegal, but his motives are pure 'nuf. Anyway, this child's daddy comes out here from time to time just to make sure the sun will break the grasp of darkness. Or, so he says.

Sparky inched closer and gently touched the tip of Hondo's long snout. "St. Francis of I-see-see loves animals. I love animals. Do you, Saryboom, love animals? Markie doesn't make the sun. But the sun listens to him."

The child paused and thought hard. "Markie sez this is not his casedral. Markie sez it is God's. Saryboom, can I ride your manatee?"

Sara laughed and hugged Sparky. Hondo snorted. "No, you can't *ride* Saryboom's manatee. Now hush, child, can't you see yer daddy's ready to begin."

A reverent quiet settled over all three…starchild, ancient one and pilgrim. Animals settled into comfortable grassy pews. The old coyote made his final adjustments on the microphone, took off his Stetson, donned a ragged set of earphones and spoke in a gruff but friendly voice.

A reverent quiet settled over all three…starchild, ancient one and pilgrim. The animals settled into comfortable grassy pews. The old coyote made his final adjustments on the microphone, took off his Stetson, donned a ragged set of earphones and spoke in a gruff friendly voice.

"This is Coyote Bill comin' to you live from the St. Francis Starlite Cathedral…with another broadcast of the Reverend Doctor Marc Purebread's sunrise worship services. This morning's musical guest is Jyssy Joshua. As always we are being brought to you by the Luchenbach Memorial Tradin' Post and Coffee House, featuring the hottest deals and squarest meals this side of the Mississippi…Remember K-SKY….Commercial-free…BS-free…Pollution-free…radio. And now, welcome to the Greatest Show on Earth, brought to you live from K-SKY radio…Voice of the free world."

Marc Purebread fiddled with his glasses and glanced at the notecards resting on the rugged stone pulpit. He tapped on the microphone and spoke.

Creator God, help us to be help-less today...

"

"Creator God, help us to be helpless today...
Cause us to need you again...
Lead us out from the crowds of self interest
to your unselfish heart.
Let us hear the voice of Jesus
so we can once more seek your face. Amen."

"Amen" from a million voices shook the valley...without a sound. Marc glanced at his child, sitting in Sara's lap. He smiled and winked.

"There once was a Sunday school class that had decided to stage the 'WORLD'S GREATEST CHRISTMAS PAGEANT.' There were more kids than parts, so their wise teacher enlarged the role of sheep in the production."

As though they understood him, many of the sheep gathered, they baa-ed. Proudly, Sara presumed. Marc nodded at them and continued.

"A six year old asked her teacher, 'What's the big deal with sheep anyway? I never even saw one.' Her world-wise classmate snapped, 'You oughta-be glad. They're fuzzy, and stupid, and scared...and...THEY STINK!'"

A sheep took audible exception to this. Marc glanced over his glasses at them. "Present company excepted. So the little girl looked at her friend and cried, 'I DON'T WANNA BE A SHEEP!'"

Marc took a sip of coffee as snickering from the goats and llamas subsided.

"Probably, if it came right down to it, all of us would all agree with the little girl. I DON'T WANNA BE A SHEEP."

A fat woodchuck, doubled over in laughter and fell off a stump. Two sheep stood to leave but were herded back by the glaring border collie. Marc looked apologetically in their direction and went on,

"When you think about it, there just isn't much of a place for sheep today. Most of us have never spent much time with them...much less owned one, even seen or touched one."

This drew approving chatter from the fold.

"And I'd imagine most of us have never met a shepherd...(mild applause). But, that little Sunday school student was right. The Bible spends a lot of time talking about them."

Two sheep stood to leave but were herded back by the glaring border collie. Marc looked apologetically in their direction and went on.

Radio listeners missed the ram's murmured, "As it should be!" Marc didn't. After a sip of coffee, he spoke a bit louder. "So what is the big deal about sheep? Yes, they are cute when they're babies (cheers), but they just follow blindly (boos), don't they? And make a big mess? And act clueless? (louder booing) And are scared all the time?"

> **'I DON'T WANNA BE A SHEEP!'"**

The flock approached rebellion until someone shouted from a rock some yards behind the preacher, "I don't wanna be a sheep!"

It was Starbuck standing beside Jyssy. Laughter rang down the valley, and the radio audience heard its soothing sound. Marc gave his eldest son a quick 'shut-up!' look and continued.

"It seems demeaning. And it certainly is difficult to find any fitting analogy to Biblical sheep or shepherds here near the end of this century. But maybe that gives Jesus' words a sharper edge, spoken so long ago at Solomon's portico in the Great Temple. 'My sheep hear my voice. I know who they are…and they follow me.'"

Silence rained down upon them all. A dust-brilliant sun waited just beneath the mountain peaks. After another sip, he spoke again.

"Events of recent times in Los Angeles are still clear in our minds.
Many voices said many things.
Many would-be leaders rose to demand,
'Follow me…hear my voice!'
Only fools and bigots assume
that those who *followed* no one in particular
into chaos and violence, before,
would not follow these leaders' voices
blindly into silence, now.

> A fat woodchuck, doubled over in laughter and fell off a stump.

"But *there* is the paradox!
There, it is!

"In a culture where respect for
leaders and institutions seems at its lowest ebb,
where faith in the system
is seen as incredible….

"Where being a follower
is regarded as weakness.
Nonetheless, all people cry out for
a strong and wise and compassionate leader…
to lead them out of Egypt to some Promised Land.

"Yet, rather than commit to a leader,
most people recoil in fear…
the fear of following.
Fear of leaving the pack,
for safety in the darkness.

"Afraid…
afraid of what the light
might reveal…"

Marc placed both hands firmly on the stone altar before him, closed his eyes tightly and shouted,

"I DON'T WANNA BE A SHEEP!!!"

The sheep whispered amongst themselves but all else was still, and he went on.

"So we remain—
Non-sheep.
Not followers.
But not quite leaders either.

"Maybe just non-sheep
Adrift in our cocoons
Craving a leader
to quietly heal our
Silent wounds.

"So we slip
Unnoticed into one crowd or another
Flowing without resistance
from one non-solution to the next…
without much argument,
Temporary followers…
over…and over again."

Only the winds far to the east made a sound.
Only the sheep seemed confused.
Only those listening heard.
Marc's voice pressed on.

"According to St. John's Gospel,
during the Festival of Dedication in Jerusalem,
Jesus walked into the temple,
and taught in Solomon's portico.

"
Silence rained down upon them all.

Afraid…
afraid of what the light
might reveal…"

"

"This Festival of Dedication is better known
to us as the Festival of Lights,
Hanukkah.

"This Festival marked
the Maccabbean Revolt of 167 B.C.
and celebrates the
cleansing of the Temple
that Gentiles had defiled.
It was symbolic of King Solomon's
cleansing of the Temple centuries earlier.

Marc paused to let a portly turkey waddle by.
It was gobbling, "Maccabbeans…what a bunch of
turkeys…gobble-ha!"

Marc paused to let a portly turkey
waddle by.

"The Maccabbeans literally faced
overwhelming odds.
But their bravery and conviction
saved Judaism's identity as God's People.

"About 200 years later,
Jews once again celebrated
who they were,
and what they believed
and what made them free…

"But there,
there on the very porch of King Solomon,
there was Almighty God on earth,
the One God in eternity now among us
as the person named Jesus.
The visible completion of all they believed.
God—Jesus—was walking among them…
But they would not believe…
They would not follow.

"Their Law, and Tradition,
and the fear of losing control.
These made them…
non-sheep."

" without much argument,
becoming followers…
over…and over again. "

He cleared this throat. Except for the "CRRREEEE" of the locusts, there
was no other sound. He glanced through the bottom of his bifocals at
worn pages on the altar and resumed softly, shifting toward full Purebread throttle.

"Non-sheep.
So long ago on Solomon's portico
they gathered around the Rabbi,
and spat their questions at him.

"'So how long are you going to
keep us hanging in suspense?
If you are the Messiah,
then, SAY IT!

"Jesus, a man of ultimate patience
must have just shaken his head
when he said,
'I told you…
and you don't believe me.
All the works I've done
in my Father's name
testify to Who I am…
but you don't believe me.
You don't believe me…
because
YOU DON'T BELONG TO MY SHEEP!'"

> "Their Law and Tradition,
> and the fear of losing control:
> These made them…
> non-sheep."
>
> "'So how long are you going to
> keep us hanging in suspense?
> If you are the Messiah,
> then, SAY IT!'"

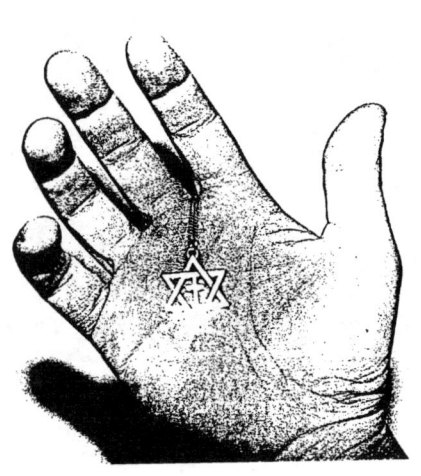

"Yessir, tell it, Doctor," an ecstatic grackle cried.
"Uh-huh, Lord, Lord," shouted one of the lambs.
"Yeah, Markie!" Sparky called.

The commotion rippled down the hillside, and he went on,

"Whose sheep were they?
I mean, this faction among the children of Israel…
Heirs of the living God…
Strong!
And proud!
Celebrating their freedom
during the Festival of Lights.
They saw Jesus,
looked at him dead in the eyes
and said,
'I DON'T WANNA BE YOUR SHEEP!'"

The last phrase caused an outcry like you'd hear in a revival tent. One of the wombats flew into a frenzy of "Amens" and "Hallelujahs" before Marc spoke again.

"So,
whose sheep
were they?"

Again, he was interrupted by noisy "Amens," "Preach it, Doctor," and variations of "Alleluias." He waited for silence and sipped more coffee. He continued in a lighter voice more suited to the dawning skies.

"A young person told me recently
that he didn't believe
in an invisible savior.
Besides, he had never heard God's voice…
Didn't even *think* God had one…
and if he ever did hear it,
he would be afraid of what that
voice might say.
So, he concluded,
he would just
have to make it on his own.

"So, that young man left our conversation,
lurching off to follow
whoever would offer human touch…
and could market their
heart…

"WHOSE SHEEP ARE THEY?"

"Tell us, Doctor, tell us," one of the band members responded.

"The poor child," a mama sheep said solemnly.

Dr. Purebread straightened himself and launched into the mike, "How…and when
does the church
rise out of our
non-confrontational…
noncommittal…
noncontroversial…
non-SHEEP
…status quo
and go to claim God's
lost sheep!? (shouted Amens, *et al*).

"And snatch them…
from harm's way?"

The audience was into his rhythm all the way now. Each phrase and pause was greeted with jubilant affirmation. He forged deeper.

I mean, this faction among the children of Israel…Heirs of the living God…
                                            "

"A young person told me recently that he didn't believe in an invisible savior."

"WHOSE SHEEP ARE THEY?"

"Tell us, Doctor, tell us," one of the band members responded.
                                            "

112

"Markie's in a bad move..."

"Maybe,
maybe when each of us asks ourself,
who...and *what*
WE are following...
Maybe if we stop acting like
GOT-IT-ALL-TOGETHER
NON-SHEEP...
And allow the Good Shepherd
to snatch us back from Satan's deception,
Maybe then..."

"Markie's in a bad move now," Sparky whispered to Sara. "He's movin' in for the kill all right," Hondo added. Marc flipped a tattered page and his voice dropped to an almost inaudible level.

"Jesus looked at those gathered
on King Solomon's porch
and he told 'em
His sheep hear his voice,
that they *know* his voice,
they RECOGNIZE it!

"And, then they follow him.

> **"**
> Maybe if we stop acting like
> GOT-IT-ALL-TOGETHER
> NON SHEEP...
> **"**

"He said,
'I give them everlasting life...
They will never ever perish
here or forever!
No one!
No one, will ever
SNATCH THEM OUT OF
MY HAND!
NO ONE!
EVER!"

By now his voice was deafening and Coyote Bill had trouble equalizing his monitors. His sidekick, Destiny Bobcat, sat on a nearby rock and chuckled. "Freedom is sweet...Tell 'em, Doc!" Marc pressed on without pause.

"TODAY...
Today there is a cry for
Freedom...
It's lifting its uncertain voice
above all human tumult...

Just look to the events in the
former Soviet Republic…
Look to Afghanistan…Peru…
the Middle East.
Look to Watts.
Look to
the inhabitants of our inner cities,
or South Central L.A.
Look at our own children
in the suburbs of America!
Look and listen…
Look to this generation."

(He was staring right at Sara Doom.)

Hondo nudged her and whispered,
"Kinda like an ole Woodstock flashback, huh?"

"This cry for human freedom,
its sounds crashing into each other.
A cacophony of need…
and of loss.
It is a cry of discovery…
and of pain.
Few will follow anyone,
for fear of losing control…
No one will listen to voices
of reason and self-sacrifice
for fear of losing power…

"So time after time,
people are snatched away.
Snatched away
by the deception
that autonomous freedom
promises…
a pseudo-peaceful soul.

"So, like Biblical sheep,
We are led astray,
time and time again….
Only to feel lost
…and helpless
…and alone…
like a sheep…
NOT FREE AT ALL…"

"Look at our own children
in the suburbs of America!
Look and listen…
Look to this generation."

"Freedom is sweet…Tell 'em, Doc!"

" Sparky stared into the distance. It was the awesome look of faith. "

" "The voice that cries 'FREEDOM—FREEDOM THROUGH FORGIVE-NESS'

The voice that cries, 'FREEDOM—FREEDOM THROUGH PEACE.'

"Maybe
that voice…" "

His voice dropped off. There was only a sound, something like a child's nestling yawn that seemed to come from somewhere over a nearby mountain as the first golden glint of sun reached them. Sara gasped. There were tears in Hondo's eyes, and in Marc's. Sparky stared into the distance. It was an awesome look of faith. Her father wiped his eyes and continued.

"The cry for freedom
on our own terms
has led to
Destruction.

"But, if there were something…
If there were someone…
Someone
who could hold us fast,
someone
who would never let us go…
someone
not listening
to who *we* think we are…

"Then maybe,
maybe
we could hear *that* voice…

"The voice
that cries 'FREEDOM—
FREEDOM THROUGH FORGIVENESS'

"The voice
that cries, 'FREEDOM—
FREEDOM THROUGH PEACE.'

"The voice
that only perfect love
can proclaim…

"Maybe
that voice…"

Something sounding like "yes" washed over the hilltops. Thousands of light particles danced skyward. A ray of light reached Marc's eyes and he squinted. He looked at his beaten-black-Bible, closed it softly, and spoke. His voice didn't quite sound like him.

"Jesus said one final thing
to those gathered on Solomon's portico.
He said,
'What God has given to me…
It is greater than anything else.'

"No one can take it out of my hand,
because no one,
no one can take it out of God's hand.
You see,
Jesus and God…
Are one…"

Marc Purebread removed his glasses and looked at a sky
 filling with light and turned to his child and smiled.

"The closest thing to a sheep I can think of
is my baby daughter…MaClain.
She's not quite three months old,
not even ten pounds yet.
She's like a little lamb.
Big bright watery eyes.
Looking out at the world
a little timid
but trusting.
A little curious,
yet cautious
and open.
Full of discovery
yet dependent,
totally unique,
but so like us all.

"Desperately,
demanding love…

"Her survival
is a result of others'
sacrifice
and care
and kindness…

"You see,
she wants to be a sheep.

"Whose voice do we hear?
Whose sheep are we?"

"She's like a little lamb.
Big bright watery eyes.
Looking out at the world
a little timid
but trusting.
Desperately,
demanding love…"

"Listen to the voice."

"No one can take it out of my hand, because no one,
no one can take it out of God's hand.
You see,
Jesus and God...
Are one..."

Sunbolts were filling the vaulted sky. Sara stood and lifted her hands to the heavens, feeling the fresh daylight's warmth on her face like it was the first time.
With tears glistening in the light, she prayed,

"Oh, thank you, Great Grandfather.
My ethic is not lost.
Thanks be to your Christ
who nailed it to your cross."

— *The Ballad of Sara Doom*

Marc acknowledged her words and went to her. Coyote Bill scrambled after him, slipping on dewy rocks to keep the mike within range. Then, Dr. Purebread concluded with his arm around Sara Doom, and with Sparky clinging to his neck,

"The world is overpopulated with non-sheep, Sara Doom.
They're out there (he pointed across the valley).
They are there,
looking for a Shepherd,
clearly asking us,
You...
and me:

'IF YOU KNOW THE ANSWER,
TELL US!
TELL US PLAINLY.
DON'T COVER IT IN
RITUAL AND PROPRIETY.
NOR HIDE IT BEHIND CATHEDRAL WALLS.
DON'T HIDE IT WITHIN
DENSE VERSES OF YOUR SONGS,
DON'T MAKE IT A GUESSING GAME
WITHOUT A RHYME.

"TELL US IN WORDS WE CAN UNDERSTAND,
IF YOU KNOW WHO THE MESSIAH IS.
SHOW US CLEARLY, NOW.
SHOW US IN YOUR OWN LIVES,
IN YOUR OWN ACTIONS.
LOOK US IN OUR EYES.
IF YOU HAVE AN ETHIC,
GIVE US
REASON TO BELIEVE IT!

"Like Sparky here
and her little sister…
Timid, but trusting,
Curious but open,
Dependent.
Desperate for love,
and healing touches,
Waiting for kindness.

"Like each dawn,
We are unique…
But so like each other.

"**WE** are all sheep."

Amens rolled over the hillside and met the advancing morning sun. "At last," thought Sara. She looked into Sparky's face. The child was absorbed by love as she looked at her father. They were speaking an unspoken language. It's the one for which Sara had been searching. And, she began to hum a quiet song.

"They're out there…
looking for a Shepherd,
clearly asking us,
You
and me."
"Like each dawn,
We are unique…
But so like each other."

"

"So afraid to look…
Are you watching me?
So afraid to see
Speak to me today.
Show me some way
(To) Help me trust you,
help me trust you."

—*The Ballad of Sara Doom*

Marc looked at her and asked, "Where did you hear that? It's beautiful!"

Sara looked directly toward the blazing morning sky.
"One of my people out there,
A girl, I think.
I will find her and tell her the
Purebread story."

"You mean the Nuclear Disaster?" Starbuck laughed.
He slapped his stepfather on the back. "Great show, Marc. Most excellent. Jyssy and the band and I are gonna drop a few numbers for K-SKY, but we'll catch ya later."

As he trotted off, the band had already begun a ripping rendition of "Amazing Grace" with Jyssy shouting to the hills,

"How sweet the sound.
That saved a wretch like meee…"

By then, Marc and company were surrounded by well-wishers. "Great sermon, Doc."
"Best yet, Marc."
"Make 'em weep, preacher."
…and so on.

"
"Like each dawn,
We are unique…
But so like each other.

"Help me to trust you…"

"You have been listening to the voice of the Free World, K-SKY radio, and Dr. Marc Purebread; now the soulful sound of Jyssy Joshua and friends."

"

Sara drank it all in. Coyote Bill was speaking into the headset and winked at Marc.

"You have been listening to the voice of the Free World, K-SKY radio, and Dr. Marc Purebread. Now the soulful sound of Jyssy Joshua and friends." The music played on. Marc bowed to the ram as he led his flock away, then turned and spoke to Sara, "It's time for you to get on with your life, Sara. But first you need to sample some of Ransom, Texas' special cookin.'"

"You were loud, Markie. Let's eat breakfast. Sparky's hungry," his daughter laughed.

And they all came down from the St. Francis Starlite Cathedral arm-in-arm. The sun wrapped its warm cloak upon their backs. Jyssy kept singing…

"…I once was lost,
but now I'm found…
was blind…
but now…
I SEE…"

And Sara Doom sang with her the song of her own generation,

"Hold my hand,
Lead the way.
Open my eyes
Just lead the way
Don't lose Faith.
(I'm trying so hard).
Trust in me."

(So ends *The Ballad of Sara Doom*)

 **SHEEP CROSSING ZONE**

Culture Zone: When you come to the place in the road where the sheep are following someone just out of view, you might get the urge to find out who.

K-SKY
© Michael O. Harrington

"...WELCOME BACK TO K-SKY, RADIO TO THE FREE WORLD...THIS IS WILD BILL COYOTE AND MY PADNER OLD DESTINY BOBCAT...WE'RE JEST BREEZIN' WITH A FEW FRIENDS...OKAY, JYSSY JOSHUA, TELL US ABOUT YER NEW RELEASE, THE BALLAD OF SARA DOOM."

THANKS Bill... The disc is NOT your run-of-the-mill set of tunes. Ya see, it's all about the *SOUL* of a Generation...

It's the VOICE, *dig?*

So WHAT makes this Whipper-Snapper DOOM the Voice of her DING-BLASTED BUNCH O' hoodlums? EH?

Don't blow an artery, old fellow...I've met Doom and heard the tune...at Doc Purebread's...But hey, let's hear from our guests. LAY IT ON ME, BIG E!

YA, Doc Purebread iz zee comic genius, ya? But oh dat kinder—SARA, she iz majic. Here we iz talkin' fuzzy fellas an de fat little armored pig...undt I'm not feelin' dead. We iz all relatives, *NO???*

Armored *PIG!?* Who let the Mark Twain look-a-like in? (It's called a hairbrush...check it out.)
Pay attention, the culture is *Clueless*, the Media are *dorks*, and Sara Doom is a *Prophet*...
LISTEN, LEARN IT,

BUY IT.

Nuff said.

120

I'M TRYING TO DATE MYSELF

Dubuque, Iowa, seems unstuck in time and space, he thought. Most people come to Iowa and expect cornfields…their Field of Dreams. But, Dubuque sits on a bend in the Mississippi, part Irish-Polish-German mining town, part river boat gambler, and part East coast turn-of-the-century charm. There are few fields here.

The Writer thumbed through his notes in a hotel room. He put them on the bed and walked over to the window. It was late at night, but there were still many young people swimming and playing hard in the motel pool. CNN was droning in the background. This report seemed to center on Americans and their heroes. He saw several football Hall of Famers' drawn faces on the screen, and then looked back to the young people clowning in the pool.

"Did you find any heroes out there, Sara? There must be some possible candidates in your generation. Mine are all worn out. I was always partial to Joe DiMaggio, but baseball has lost its poetry these days. At my age, it's okay for me to long for the 'good old days,' but don't you do it…yours haven't been written yet, and your poetic game is still a dream."

He picked up the phone and dialed his wife, "Hi babe. What am I doing? Oh, not much…Guess I'm trying to date myself…"

Joltin' Joe has come and gone…

 **STRIKE ZONE**

Culture Zone: Heroes often go on strike…our dreams miss the fast balls of reality thrown at them at 90 MPH, sometimes even our poetry strikes out…but the game will not be called on account of pain.

EPILOGUE

"MAKE IT SO!"

Before Sara left the Purebreads, she joined them for breakfast and saw for herself what Starbuck had named a "Nuclear Disaster." The kitchen table was a solid oak slab laden under enough food for the Fifth Army. It was surrounded by a dozen or so assorted chairs and two antique hardwood baby chairs. Since all seats were taken, Starbuck was sitting on a counter by the stove and a few other folks were standing around, plates in hand. The commotion was somewhere between rush hour traffic and a jostled beehive. Just the noise generated by utensils would have driven most persons screaming into the night. But it was a happy sound. It was the sound of safety and place, and being with people you can count on.

> **But it was a happy sound. It was the sound of safety and place, and being with people you can count on.**

The following is a brief synopsis of comments sent Sara's way amidst the comforting chaos. (Much more and you might not believe it.)

"I'll tell you what being a Purebread means. It means hand-me-downs from your older brothers…and shut-me-ups from your older sisters. And less TV time."

—*Wild Bill Purebread* (age 13)

"Being a Purebread means: Never having to say pass me some more cake…'cause there isn't any."

—*Thomas Purebread* (age 18)

"Being a Purebread means: 'Watch your little sister…'"

—*Doll Purebread* (age 9)

> **"I'll tell you what being a Purebread means. It means hand-me-downs from your older brothers…and shut-me-ups from your older sisters. And less TV time."**

"Being a Purebread means: Finding your favorite blue jeans on your sons, and your lucky tee shirts on your daughters, and your toothbrush being used in the dog's mouth."

—*Marc Purebread* (age 45)

"No-no-no, being with this crowd means someone bleached your new jeans, and shrank your shirts, and threw the toothbrush out with the dogs."

—*Starbuck* (age 21)

"Very funny. Being a Purebread means: Trying to discover who has made the most disgusting mess—the animals or the boys."

—*Autumn Purebread* (age 24)

122

"Dad, he's weird!"

"ThhpPHtt"

"You see, my fishes, Saryboom. That's Spot and that's Bob. I'm sorry, but you cannot have them."

—*Sparky Purebread* (age 2)

"It's cool. Can I have some bacon?"

—*Wild Bill*

"Dad, he's *weird*!"

—*Doll*

"Thhpftt!"

—*McClain Purebread* (3 months)

"It's learning to share with others."

—*Skipper Purebread* (age 40 something)

"Right, let's get mushy about it."

—*Starbuck* (again)

"It means sarcasm equals survival."

—*Thomas*

"Phhtt-thppht!"

—*McClain*

"What it means is: Oh gross! Look what they're letting the baby do with that pancake, Mother!"

—*Autumn*

"Where's my sports section? Honey?"

—*Marc*

"Right under your spilled coffee. It means: Grateful children who are concerned about others' feelings."

—*Skipper*

"Right Mom—the Guilt Thing is good in front of company."

—*Starbuck*

"Being a Purebread means: Much laughter and caring."

—*Poncho* (fifty something)

LEAVE-IT-TO-BEAVER ZONE (*AKA:* FAMILY ZONE)

Culture Zone: The image of the nuclear family may be a bit skewed these days, but the Cleavers are still out there and being with them still feels good. By the way, your people (whoever they are) fit this image, too.

"You see, Sara, the nuclear family as America's norm is becoming history. It's outta here. By the next century it could be a dinosaur. Marriage, divorce, remarriage, live-ins, alternative life styles, and on it goes. "Normal" is becoming a blended family thing. Dig this, we got a yours-mine-ours-and theirs kind of gig in this home. As far as making it a nuclear thing, well it would be a disaster. But, this thing's happenin'. Because of Mom and Marc. But us, too. It's a sacrifice. But hey, what ain't?"

That would be—*Starbuck*

"Being a Purebread is Me!

—"I'm *Sparky*."

As a kind of Breakfast Benediction, there were many hugs and, "Come back soon," and exchanges of many treasures (like rocks and beaded handmade things), and some tears. Skipper led Sara outside Ransom to the Welcome sign.

"Wait here, Sara," she said. "Starbuck tells me your ride will be along soon." She turned to leave, then stopped and smiled. "Sara Doom. Tell your generation one thing from a mom. Tell them there's always a warm bed and hot food in Ransom for them. Tell them someone does care." She waved and was gone.

Sara stood in the bright sunlight. She did not mind waiting now. There was a rustling in the brush. It was Hondo. He paused and winked.

"Well, Princess, seems you found that lost ethic of yours. Never was altogether gone, though. But you never know…. If someone don't tell someone, it might not stick around."

Sara bent down on one knee and placed her hand on the old 'dillo's head.

"Bless you, Sir Hondo. The story goes with me."

"I'm off to Austin. The band has a recording session with Jyssy Joshua. Something called, *The Ballad of Sara Doom*. I figure I better be there to keep 'em outta trouble. Besides, there's been some reports of the sun not shinin' and I wanna check it out. Who knows, might see ya in those parts. Vaya con dios, Señorita."

Sara knelt on the ground and watched him leave. He said over his shoulder,

"Looks like yer ride is here. Happy Trails."

And he was gone.

She looked up as an oversized silver RV stopped beside her. The doors opened with an hydraulic swoosh and a striking bald man spoke to her.

"Ah yes, you must be Sara Doom, Princess of the Dawn. Our friends, the Purebreads, asked us to give you a lift. It seems we are headed your way. Please join our crew."

"Tell your generation one thing from a mom to you all. Tell them there's always a warm bed and some hot food in Ransom for them. Tell them someone does care." She waved and was gone.

"

"Happy Trails"

"And where is home, Sara?"

"Home is…home is the Badlands of South Dakota," Sara remembered at last. "Is that out of your way?"

Sara picked up her knapsack and stepped on board. Inside, the RV looked like the Bridge of the Starship Enterprise. She was greeted by a beautiful woman with long dark hair who took her bag. Her manner seemed to say, "Welcome, child." Sara was seated and her host addressed the driver, "Engage."

"Aye, Captain," replied a handsome young Black man with odd sunglasses.

The vehicle flew through the Hill Country. Sara looked back at Ransom and could see Sparky and some of her siblings chasing about with their dogs. She looked at the 'Captain.'

"I am going home, sir…Captain," she said.

"And where is home, Sara," the man asked with a rich unknown accent.

"Home is…home is the Badlands of South Dakota," Sara remembered at last. "Is that out of your way?"

The 'Captain' spoke with firmness to a tall man with a close-cropped beard.

"Are the Badlands on our way, Number One? Or do we need to alter our course?"

"The coordinates are already fixed, Captain. At your command," said the man called Number One.

"Then make it so. Sara and I have much to discuss about her mission," the Captain said.

"Make it so," whispered Sara.

The driver turned on the radio. Sara was served a hot beverage and rich cakes. She and the Captain were in deep discussion. The radio announcer said,

"This is Coyote Bill with a special dedication to the Invisible Generation…

"This one's goin' out with love from Jyssy, Starbuck, Hondo and the gang,

"Hang onto yer hats, folks, for the World Premiere performance of *THE BALLAD OF SARA DOOM.*

"Comin' at ya live via someone's satellite from K-SKY radio, the voice of the Free World."

And Jyssy sang on… ♪ ♫

*"There is a code of silence
among Native American survivors, I suppose.
It may be the hurt that comes from a trust that never was
…or one long broken.
Within this ancient quiet waits a secret hope.
It trembles to awaken.
Ageless as the Badlands' stones under a weary traveler's feet,
the secrets of silence wait.
Because they have no choice.*

*"Oh listen, Spirit Master, to an ocean roar of stones.
Like stars that fell to earth scattered without design.
The children of this planet are becoming hard to find.
From the Badlands of Dakota
Sara Doom will soon see that
the eyes of all God's children
look just like you and me."*

—*The Ballad of Sara Doom*

 **GENERATION ZONE**

Culture Zone: It really is your generation…and your voice…your future where none of you (or anyone else) has gone before…MAKE IT SO!

"This is **MY** ship!"

"That is illogical, Captain."

"Let **ME** deal with the older generat

(Dubuque, Iowa, the next night) He came back from the board meeting "Black Irish tired," as his dad used to say. (This is feeling like you've been digging up potatoes all day and hanging out with a militant movement, all at the same time.) He was too tired to write—much less think—and flipped on the motel room TV. After calling room service for a pot of coffee, he went to the table and stared at his notebook.

"What's lacking today is a good sense of humor," he said out loud. From across the room he watched a movie about a half-breed Viet Nam vet in the Southwest who took a stand for an Indian Reservation school. It took The Writer back to his college days. Without noticing, he was speaking the movie's dialogue with the character.

"No man, you blew it. I felt nothing for you as a robber.'"

Turning to his victim, the bystander spoke (and so did The Writer).

"You hold on there, because I'll be robbing you in a minute."

Again to the would-be robber and real-life cop, and the bystander said (with The Writer),

"There's an honest tax-paying citizen ready to blow his foot off because you have failed to take control of the situation, like… DROP THE GUN AND UP AGAINST THE WALL."

Just then, his coffee arrived. The teenage waiter looked at the TV while The Writer searched for a tip. The waiter said, "Hey, I know that movie. It's a cult classic, *Billy Jack,* produced by the National Student Film Association in the early seventies. Cool flick. I'm taking film at the college.

"Yeah, those old films were something. I mean, see the microphone. Almost every scene, they couldn't hide the boom mikes. Can you believe that? And the plot was so classic, ya know, Indian warrior takes on the white man. And all that folk music."

"Bill."

"Make it so."

he Writer handed the young man a five and smiled, "You know, I've bably seen it 45 times. My favorite line is when Billy Jack tells Jean 'Everything they want from here on out, they're gonna have to take.'"

iter looked embarrassed and said, "Sure…um thanks for the tip, 's your receipt, Sir. Hope you enjoy your movie."

vatched the young man walk away down the hall, and smiled him laugh.

"See, I told you we needed a little humor and surprise," he said and closed the door.

He poured himself a cup of coffee and sat down. He looked at the scene on the TV and thought about the young waiter. He laughed to himself and began to write.

"Into forever night
And the teeth of the beast,
Shines a deathless light.
Jesus is laughing."

— *The Ballad of Sara Doom*

"

"Into forever night
And the teeth of the beast,
Shines a deathless light.
Jesus is laughing."

"

 **LAUGHING ZONE**

Culture Zone: Finding the place where laughter is created.

HAWKEYE AND ME

Sometimes late at night, The Writer cannot write (or sleep or hope)…so he places an old M*A*S*H* rerun tape into the VCR. The images of Hawkeye, Radar, and Hot Lips never lose their warmth, their humor, their humanity.

"Each person needs to be able to look into a dark mirror at themselves and see friendly faces looking back at them and encouraging them to press on through the pathos and futility of human struggle," he mused out loud.

Why does Hawkeye inspire me, he wondered. "Late at night I guess we both are tending wounded souls and plotting ways to beat the system," he heard himself answer.

He turned up the volume, and his old friend spoke. "I don't know why they're shooting at us. All we want to do is bring them democracy and white bread; to transplant the American dream: Freedom, achievement, hyper-acidity, affluence, flatulence, technology, tension, the inalienable right to an early coronary at your desk while plotting to stab your boss in the back."

The Writer laughed, "Preach it, Doctor!"

 **AFTER-M*A*S*H* ZONE**

Culture Zone: After the last episode of each stage in your life comes that feeling of loss till an old friend pushes the rerun button and you see things with new eyes and hear new voices all over again and again.

POSTSCIPT

"FROM THE BADLANDS, WITH LOVE"

Sara sat cross-legged across the fire from Wally Skydancer. He puffed on his eagle bone pipe and spoke.

"So, what did you learn, Princess of Dawn?"

I felt the voices of my brothers
and my sisters
Crying in the land of Watts…
Standing on the mountains,
Waiting for a chance
To be heard.

> *"I learned that things are not*
> *altogether lost (or as they seem)*
> *after you find them.*
> *I found Faith in Sparky's eyes,*
> *And heard Purebread children sing.*
> *It was the sound of*
> *Gratitude.*
> *The ancient one, Hondo,*
> *helped me laugh at myself*
> *because we are so frail (being human, of course).*
>
> *I felt the voices of my brothers*
> *and my sisters*
> *Crying in the land of Watts,*
> *Standing on the mountains*
> *Waiting for a chance*
> *To be heard.*
>
> *On my way, I have been surrounded by God's angels.*
> *And I've seen the face of one*
> *called Christ."*
> — The Ballad of Sara Doom

"Sara, you have, indeed, found that *most* excellent thing!"

Wally Skydancer smiled and continued,

"But tell me, my child—where is your *ethic*?"

She pointed to her heart.

She pointed to her heart.

 **ALPHA-AND-OMEGA ZONE**
We think we have a beginning and an end…but God doesn't.

GROUND
THOUGHTS ON THE BALLAD

BY DR. MARC PUREBREAD

(The Writer went to an excellent seminary. Here's some proof:)

Adamah (ah-dah-mah') is a Hebrew word that appears 225 times in the Old Testament and means arable, cultivable land. That meaning can be seen in the expression "man of *adamah*" meaning "farmer" (Gen. 9:20; Zech. 13:5). *Adamah* and its synonym *afar* ("dust ground") are the material from which God forms the first man (*adam*; Gen. 2:7; 3:19; Ps. 90:3; Job 10:9; 34:15). In addition to this primary meaning, *adamah* can signify the inhabited world (Gen. 12:3: 28:14; Deut. 7:6; 14:2; Isa. 24:21; Amos 3:2), the land God gives to Israel in fulfillment of his oath to the patriarchs (esp. Deut. 5:6; 7:13; 11:9; 26:10, 15), from which they are exiled (2 Kings 17:23; 25:21) and to which they return.

" It is ground zero of the nuclear family's holocaust. This holocaust has taken shape and form over the past forty years. "

Today there seems to be grounds for despair about the church's future. There are grounds today for feeling helpless because we have not reached this younger generation. *They* are our hope and our ground. These times are ground zero for the nuclear family's holocaust. This holocaust is the monstrous offspring conceived on Ego's altar for the past forty years. A holocast that counterfeits the hopes and dreams of what was best about this land. The hopes and dreams of our fathers and mothers and their fathers and mothers, reaching back to when their bold ancestors set foot on the shores of this Promised Land.

I cannot picture there being no viable church by the time our generation turns 50, 60, and 70. I cannot imagine there being no place of comfort for our children and their children. But these kids, this generation, have been ground like hamburger. A time bomb threatens their hopes and dreams—the politics of greed and our lust for more than our fair portion of this creation. These kids are not as much lost as they are foundlings of a future lacking basic principles we claim. So they find themselves clinging to each other, listening to each other, holding onto each other because the inheritance we would give them either binds them in the twine of our expectations or melts in their inexperienced hands like lies. But the principles and decision-making approaches that they do bring to the table of human experience are filled with the wonder of new possibilities. And the ground on which they move so tenatively trembles ever so slightly, as if expecting and hoping beyond hope that this generation will become the one to reform a planet that equity, and charity, and love will find hospitable.

But these kids, this generation, are being ground like hamburger. A time bomb threatens their hopes and dreams, the politics of greed, and our lust for more than our fair portion of this creation.

"

FOUR DECADES OF FAILURE PRELUDE FRESH DENOMINATIONAL MODELS OF YOUTH MINISTRY

The church invests a lot of hope in these young people. But it keeps spinning dials to find the right combination to that safe ground, which we so loosely label "youth ministry." If we populate this ground with notions alien to our historic understanding of belief, justice, peace, and humility, that ground turns into swamp land. Somewhere between the paradoxes of the sacred and the profane within this generation lies the dust waiting for the breath of life.

This generation has not yet heard Ruth's voice. It is to them we must say, "Where *you* go, I will go. Your people will be my people, and your God my God"—and not the other way around. From our example they discern the outcomes of two thousand years of mud-slinging. In our arms they have found little solace. In our words they barely hear the promise. So how can we be so sure they will see Christ in our eyes, the Father in our hearts, or the Holy Spirit alive in our ways? Because Jesus stands with these young ones and identifies with their cry, the rest of us must stand with them. And in that standing, we are established on holy ground.

What this Ballad proposes is a search for holy ground. It preludes fresh denominational models for youth ministry to millions of teenagers who fall outside the types we see in churches today—those teenagers who are marginalized by our society, whether by race, abuse, or neglect. Those haunted children who choose a path that does not lead toward the mediocrity that we expect for success. A legitimate denominational youth model can only be found in concert with this generation's environmental, ethnic, educational, and artistic expectations. These are grounds for this effort. Let us resolve to heed their voice, even when it seems to be a haunting and distant echo of those things we have lost in ourselves. Let us hear with new clarity, and claim them for Christ's life and ministry through the church."

Because Jesus stands with them and identifies with their cry, the rest of us must stand with them. And in that standing, we are established on holy ground.

Teens who are marginalized by our society, whether by race, abuse, or neglect. Those haunted children who choose a path that does not lead toward the mediocrity that we expect for success.

"BEAM ME BACK, SCOTTY!"

"I canna do it, Captain. I dunna have the POWER!"

"SCOTTY'S *right*. He *doesn't* have the power. But, YOU do."

THESE ARE YOUR MARKERS

i. There is one God.

ii. Idols are very heavy things.

iii. No one else has your name.

iv. Each day is either a gift or a curse.

v. You are a source of credit to your family.

vi. Extreme prejudice is deadly.

vii. You will never be so grateful as when someone rescues you from your culture.

iix. If they take away your heart... you're helpless.

ix. Don't buy someone else's reality.

x. There is one God.

"Inevitably you will get caught in many ZONES...and you'll find it nearly impossible to get back to that EXCELLENT THING (your center—yourself, your God).

So when you *do* get stuck in a Zone...don't count on someone else to beam you back. Look for the MARKERS back to the EXCELLENT THING."

FOR EXAMPLE:
"Say you find yourself stuck in the DISCO ZONE, look for MARKER 7 to get back home."

ZERO ZONE

GET REAL ZONE

OZONE

WAR ZONE

BONGO ZONE

CRATER ZONE

NO-NAME ZONE

ALONE ZONE

END ZONE

x

i   ii

iii

ix

EXCELLENT THING SANCTUARY

iv

ME-TV ZONE

iix

NOW ZONE

FIRE ZONE

vii   vi

v

HARD ZONE

STAR ZONE

END ZONE

BOZONE

DISCO ZONE

THEOLOGY ZONE

P.S. "Try not to cling onto a Zone. Others have marked the way out." —M. Purebread

CLING ON

CULTURE ZONE INDEX

CULTURE ZONE: YOU are the prophets of your generation, naming your mission and creating your sanctuary.

GENERATION ZONE: It really is **YOUR** generation...and your voice ...your future where none of you (or anyone else) has gone before...MAKE IT SO!

ME-TV ZONE: That sneaking suspicion that you are on some really bad reality TV show without a laugh track. p. 52

NO APARTHEID ZONE: That most miraculous of places where forgiveness outweighs hatred and humility makes the sun shine. p. 86

NO CROSSING ZONE: We choose not to cross borders we've made because we fear what lies between there and here. p. 98

NO IDOLIZING ZONE: It's a quiet place where you shut off your engine long enough to get a good idea. p.38

NO LOITERING ZONE: Feeling like there's no place to hang while you wait. p. 24

NO NAME ZONE: Without a name—you're nothing. p.41

NO PARKING ZONE: Here's a tip—when everything feels worthless, make sure nobody tries to pick your pocket. p 30

NO SMOKING ZONE: That odd perspective that all that separates your section from the smoking zone is an outstretched arm holding a lit match. p. 32

NO SWIMMING ZONE: The feeling that it's not the ocean that's toxic. p.58

NO TALKING ZONE: Ssshh! Be quiet! Someone may hear you, or you may hear them. p. 25

NO TIME ZONE: Too much information with no application. p. 45

NOW ZONE: Being in the moment when whatever you do is okay. p. 21

NUCLEAR-FREE ZONE: The sense that Nuclear Disaster is not just a bygone theory and making yourself feel better by thinking it's gone. p. 23

OUTTA-HERE ZONE: This is too much…bye, bye…I'm history…I'm outta-here. p. 54

OZONE: Sometimes people and situations seem just so bizarre that they draw us in. p. 54

POVERTY ZONE: The place where the poor in spirit should gather to feed the hungry. p. 48

PYRAMID ZONE: Even ancient structures sometimes leave one feeling God-forsaken. p. 39

ROUTE-66-SPEED ZONE: That feeling like you are in a black and white TV drama series, endlessly slowing down in hopes of running across your culture. p. 62

SANCTUARY ZONE: Close your eyes and imagine that perfect place of safety, warmth, and well being…yes, it is the place where your voice is born…it is the zone of worship. p. 104

SHEEP-CROSSING ZONE: When you come to the place in the road where the sheep are following someone just out of view, you might get the urge to find out who. p. 118

SHOW'S-OVER ZONE: Time after time, we find ourselves at the big show, the long-waited-for-moment, and we want to take our picture and move along to the next entertainment destination…but after we're gone, the show goes on. p.88

SONIC-BOOM ZONE: You can move as fast as you want from there to here, but eventually sound will catch up with you and…BOOM! p. 72

STAR ZONE: No, not Elvis and Madonna…you know the big star…a place where it might begin. p. 49

STRIKE ZONE: Heroes often go on strike…our dreams miss the fast balls of reality thrown at them at 90 MPH, sometimes even our poetry strikes out…but the game will not be called on account of pain. p. 120

TAKE-OFF ZONE: It's like when you feel you've got all the right stuff you need, but you ache to find some other stuff. So you just take off. p. 64

THEOLOGY ZONE: It is that one 'OLOGY' that really bakes our biscuits…no one gets it. Except every-so-often we get a piece of God's mind, even in chapel. p. 93

TIME ZONE: Since we've evolved into hurry-up-this-will-only-last-as-long-as-I-am-around Zonies…there is a lingering sense that we missed…something. p. 84

TRUE-VALUE ZONE: The feeling you get with a left and right hook. Duck! p. 31

TWILIGHT ZONE: That uneasy sense that what is eternal is too far away, and what is history never happened. p. 29

WAR ZONE: Not merely a place of conflict, but a place to take a stand. p. 52

ZERO ZONE: Being less than Zero and searching for God out there. p. 22

ZONED OUT: Being with people as nutty as you feel. p. 16

A CULTURE ZONE: SOMETHING NOT TO GET 'STUCK' IN, BUT TO BE CONSCIOUS OF… ESPECIALLY WHEN IT'S A ZONE THAT CONTRADICTS YOUR ETHIC, MARKERS, AND YOUR MOST EXCELLENT THING.

Michael O. Harrington, an ordained Lutheran pastor, has worked as a youth minister for over 20 years in multi-cultural ecumenical settings. Michael is on the Advisory Board of Wartburg Theological Seminary's Center for Youth Ministries, has been a board member of "Save our Children" and was co-founder of the San Antonio Peacemaking Conference on Gang Violence. He has been a contributor to several national publications.

Harrington has been an instructor of World Religions at St. Edward's University and has developed a course on Cultural Analysis in the Christian Context. He was an independent publicist and public relations consultant and is a sought-after speaker and seminar leader on youth culture.

For four decades he has been a self-styled "cultural cartoonist" and will soon unleash K-SKY© on the free world.

Michael and his wife, Janett, live in the Texas Hill Country with their children, two dogs, cats, assorted birds, an iguana, and a Quaker parrot named Kermit.

…And, lucky for us, Michael is a gifted spinner of tales.

For Information about author's speaking engagements or seminars, you may call 1-800-864-1648.

To Order Copies

If unavailable in local bookstores, LangMarc will fill your order within 24 hours.

Telephone Orders: Call 1-800-864-1648

Postal Orders: LangMarc Publishing, P.O. 33817, San Antonio, TX 78265-3817. USA.

The Ballad of Sara Doom
Soft cover $14.95

Quantity Discounts: 10% discount for 3-4 copies, 15% for 5-9 copies; 20% for 10 or more copies.

Shipping: Add $1.50 for 1 book (4th class); 50 cents each for additional book. Priority for 1-2 books=$2.90.

Sales tax: Texas residents, add 7.75% ($1.15)

Send a Gift to a Friend: We will mail directly. Shipping cost to each address will be $3.00 UPS or $1.50 Book Rate.

Please send payment with order.

_____ books @ $14.95 _____

Less discount (above) _____

Total book cost _____

Sales tax (TX res. 7.75%) _____

Add Shipping: _____

Check enclosed: _____

Your Name and Address for UPS or postal delivery:

LangMarc Publishing
P.O. Box 33817
San Antonio, TX 78265-3817

Your phone number: _____

Thank you for your order.